"But, Mr. [...]

"Call me Mitch. [...] you how relieved
I am to know that both you and your dog are there. I worry
about my kids. I want them to grow into loving, responsible
adults, so I'm glad you'll be taking them to church with you.
I'm definitely planning to go along myself the next time I can
wangle a Sunday off." He paused. "Oh, I'm sorry, you started
to say something and I interrupted you."

Tassie blew out her cheeks in frustration. From the sound
of it, he'd had a really rough day, too, maybe even rougher
than hers, and he was going to have to stay awake all night.
How could she add to his troubles by announcing that she
was quitting and moving out the first thing in the morning?

JOYCE LIVINGSTON loves to write and feels writing inspirational romance is her God-given ministry. A wife, mother, grandmother, and former television broadcaster, she has many life experiences from which to draw. Her books have won numerous awards, including Heartsong's Contemporary Author of the Year in 2003 and 2004, and Book of the Year numerous times. She has well over twenty books in print and more contracted and in the writing stage.

Books by Joyce Livingston

HEARTSONG PRESENTS

Don't miss out on any of our super romances. Write to us at the following address for information on our newest releases and club information.

Heartsong Presents Readers' Service
PO Box 721
Uhrichsville, OH 44683

Or visit www.heartsongpresents.com

The Preacher
Wore a Gun

Joyce Livingston

Heartsong Presents

As with every book I write, this book is dedicated to Don Livingston, my dear husband who went to be with our Lord in October 2004.

I also want to dedicate it to my pastor, Dale Lewis, of Wichita, Kansas. He is not only my pastor but also my Sunday School teacher, my friend, my mentor, and my encourager. He visits the sick and sorrowing in our church congregation daily, praying for them as only he can. Dale's ministry is truly a calling from God. His sweet words, his gentle touch, and his far-reaching prayers have impacted many hearts. He is an example of a true man of God. Dale, we appreciate and love you. Stay just as you are.

A note from the Author:
I love to hear from my readers! You may correspond with me by writing:

Joyce Livingston
Author Relations
PO Box 721
Uhrichsville, OH 44683

ISBN 978-1-60260-101-7

THE PREACHER WORE A GUN

Our mission is to publish and distribute inspirational products offering exceptional value and biblical encouragement to the masses.

PRINTED IN THE U.S.A.

one

"You didn't."

After switching her cell phone to her other ear, Tassie Springer sat down in the worn floral upholstered chair she had rescued out of a Dumpster eight years ago when she graduated from high school and moved to Omaha to enter college, nearly broke, tired, and discouraged. All she knew back then was that she wanted to leave Grand Island to get as far away as she could from the memory that plagued her day and night. Attending college in Omaha seemed to be the only logical and acceptable excuse she could use to get out of town—and away from *him*.

"Yeah, Mom, I did. I quit. My boss accused me of lying when I stood up for another employee. Considering the six faithful years I had worked for him after dropping out of college, he should have known I'd never lie, so I quit."

"So—what are you going to do now?"

Tassie swung her jean-covered leg atop the footstool then rested her head on the crocheted doily she had placed on the chair's headrest to cover a torn spot in the fabric. "At this point I'm not sure what I'm going to do, although I have come up with several options."

"You could come back to Grand Island."

Tassie patted her knee then waited until Goliath, the big black Lab she had rescued from the Humane Society, rested his big head there, his eyes focusing on her as if she were the queen of his life. "I've considered that. I may live in Omaha but Grand Island has always been my home. I've never wanted to admit it, Mom, but I made a big mistake, dropping out of college after my sophomore year to take that low-paying job. I was just tired of going to school all day and working nights and weekends babysitting my neighbor's three children while she worked. Then, with having to wedge in study time, my grades went into a downward spiral. I guess I was overstressed and suffered a burnout. If I was going to drop out of college, I should have come back home then, instead of taking that dead-end day job at the photo shop. I much preferred the babysitting but, unfortunately, it just didn't pay enough."

"I—I wish your father and I could have paid for your college but the money just wasn't there at that time."

Tassie crinkled up her face. She had only meant to explain, not accuse. "I know, Mom. I never expected you to pay my way."

"If you really want to finish your education why don't you come back and attend the University of Nebraska in Kearney, live here with your father and me, and drive back and forth? It's only a fifty-mile trip. You might even be able to find a ride. A lot of Grand Island residents go to UN Kearney."

"Funny you should mention that. I've been seriously thinking that very thing. Coming home would solve a lot of my problems."

"Your father and I are in a little better financial position now than we were back then, so we could help with some of your college expenses."

"No, Mom. I'm a big girl. Twenty-six years old to be exact. If I can't make it on my own, I shouldn't even try."

"Just remember, we're here if you need us, financially or in any other way. The spring flowers in the garden are beginning to bloom and you always liked to help with the gardening. Think what fun we could have together."

"You do make moving back sound enticing."

Her mom responded with a laugh. "I hope so. I am trying

to entice you, and this time of year would be the perfect time to make a new start. It would be so good to have you home again. Your room is sitting there just like you left it."

"You know, Mom, other than a few friends at the church I attend, I have no real ties to Omaha, especially now that I am out of a job. I've already checked. If I did enroll in the school's Kearny division, all of my credits would transfer. I've always wanted to pursue a career in hospital or healthcare management and the Kearney branch has a Bachelor of Science degree in that field."

Smiling, she clutched the phone even tighter. "Let me reweigh all the options overnight and pray about it again, and if I come to the conclusion I think I will, you can put the light on in my bedroom, Mom. If I decide to come, I'll be there in no more than two days." She could almost see her mother's beaming face on the other end of the line.

"Oh, my precious daughter, you have no idea how happy this makes me. I can't wait to tell your father there's a chance you'll be coming home. He'll be as excited as I am." Her mother's voice fairly chirped with joy, which made Tassie feel absolutely wonderful, a feeling she hadn't had in a long time. It was always nice to know you were loved. Who said you couldn't go home again?

As Tassie stood and told her mother good-bye, Goliath jumped to his feet, eyeing her quizzically.

"If I do decide to go you're going to love Grand Island, Goliath. My parents have a huge fenced-in backyard. You'll be able to run to your heart's content and not be cooped up in this stuffy apartment all day. Wouldn't that be nice?"

Goliath, apparently not understanding her words, walked nonchalantly away.

two

"Stop! That's breakable!" Mitchell Drummond grabbed for the lovely crystal vase as it tumbled from the table but he was too late. It hit the floor and shattered into a zillion pieces.

"No, don't step in it, Babette. Sit on the sofa or go to your room. I don't want you to get hurt." He gazed at the broken shards, not exactly sure how to go about cleaning them up. Rather than do as she was told, his four-year-old daughter made straightaway for the pile of broken glass and began to stomp it with her feet.

"Babette, stop!"

When she failed to heed his warning and continued to tromp through the broken glass in her pink ballet slippers, he grabbed onto her arms, lifted her up, and firmly set her on a nearby chair. "Stay there and don't move until I say you can."

She gazed at him for a moment then slid off the chair and once again began to tromp through the glass, pounding her little feet into the shards as if trying to break them into even smaller pieces.

About to explode with anger, Mitchell grabbed at her, tugged her out of the shattered mess, and held her in his arms. "Didn't you hear Daddy? Daddy doesn't want his baby girl to get hurt. You have to stay out of the glass!"

She tried to wiggle free but he held her fast.

"Let me go."

"No, not until you promise to stay out of the glass." *Promise,* he thought. *I'm asking a four-year-old to make a promise when I'm not even sure she knows what the word means.* Turning, he carefully lowered her onto the sofa. "Be a good girl. Sit there, pumpkin, and watch Daddy till he gets all the pieces into the trash can, okay?"

But his pumpkin apparently didn't like the idea of sitting and waiting. Instead, she jumped off the sofa and right into the pile of broken glass again, giving him a defiant look that made him sick to his stomach.

"Dad! You broke that ugly vase?"

Mitch turned as his thirteen-year-old son sauntered into the room, wearing his athletic shoes with the cleats in the soles and swinging his bat. "It wasn't ugly. It was expensive, and don't wear those shoes in the house, Tony. They'll tear up our hardwood floors. And quit swinging that bat before you break something."

Tony pointed to what was left of the vase. "Me break something? Looks like you already did. Don't yell at me!"

"I didn't break it. Babette did."

A smirk crossed the young boy's face. "You're blaming a little girl?"

Babette pointed to her father. "I didn't break it. Daddy did."

"Yes, you did; I saw you!" Mitch felt like a heel when Babette began to cry.

"You're a mean old daddy. I hate you. I don't want you for a daddy!" Crossing her arms over her slim chest, she spun around and headed for her room, wailing all the way.

"Now look, you made her cry."

His anger flaring, Mitch glared at his son and pointed to Tony's feet. "Didn't I tell you not to wear those shoes in the house? That's it, Tony! You're grounded and no TV or baseball games for the next two days!"

Tony huffed then swung the bat over his head, barely missing the ceiling light fixture. "And who is going to be home to make sure I stay grounded? You're always off working on a case, and Grandma lets me do anything I want."

"Not this time, young man. I'll give her specific instructions as to what you can and cannot do!"

Tony let loose a belly laugh. "As long as she has her booze she doesn't care what I do."

"Your grandmother told me she wasn't drinking anymore."

"Oh, yeah, as if you can believe her any more than you could Mom."

"Leave your mother out of this."

"You're the one who always talks about her, not us kids," Tony shot back.

"Go to your room—now!" Mitch gestured toward the stairs, his hand shaking with anger. "And don't come out for the rest of the day, do you hear me?"

Tony shrugged. "Ha! Yes, Father. Anything you say, Father."

Mitch watched as his son headed up the stairs toward his room, swinging his bat from side to side as he walked, banging it into the walls. *I've tried so hard. Where have I gone wrong?*

He cleaned up the remains of the expensive vase he had bought for his wife the last Christmas she had been with them, then moved into the garage where he emptied the shards into the large trash container.

After making sure the floor was squeaky clean, he headed up the stairs to apologize to both Tony and Babette. But when he reached his daughter's room and found her curled up on her bed, fast asleep, her thumb in her mouth, he quietly closed the door.

He moved on down the hall then, ignoring the Do Not Enter sign with its skull and crossbones, and pushed the door open a crack. "Can I come in, son?"

When Tony didn't answer, Mitch rubbed his forehead. Should he go in? Invade the boy's privacy?

"Tony?"

No answer.

"Tony, are you there?" *Maybe he decided to take a shower.* But he hadn't heard the water running when he had passed the hall bathroom the kids shared.

He carefully widened the crack and peered inside.

Tony was gone—probably climbed out his window and headed to a friend's house. If this was the first time he'd done such a thing, Mitch would have been worried. Unfortunately, this disappearing act was nothing new when it came to his son, or his oldest daughter.

❧

Three days later, Tassie threw herself onto her bed and gazed up at the huge poster-sized picture of her and her three best friends taken during their grade school years. She remembered how upset her father had been when he discovered she had thumbtacked it to her bedroom ceiling. Later that day, when her friends had come over, all four had stretched out on her bed, giggling at their images, trying to decide which one was the cutest, which one was the ugliest, and which one had the prettiest teeth. That last question had made them all laugh since all four had been wearing ugly braces at the time.

What dreams and lofty goals she'd had back then. How could she have let those things slip from her fingers like that? If she would have been stronger, able to say no when she should have, would things have been different? But she hadn't been strong. She'd been weak and that weakness would be bothering her the rest of her life.

"Tassie?"

Tassie rubbed at a tear before turning to face her mother. "Yeah, Mom, come in. I was just lying here—reminiscing."

"Supper will be ready in a few minutes. By the way, I got a big bone for Goliath from the butcher when I went to the store this morning. He's out in the backyard, having the time of his life chewing on it."

Tassie pulled herself to a sitting position, folded her legs, then wrapped her arms around her knees. "Thanks, Mom. That was really thoughtful of you. I know you don't like animals in the house but. . ."

Her mom waved a hand at her. "Don't give it another thought. A lot of my ideas have gone by the wayside since you've been away. Times have gotten so much worse, even in a peaceful city like Grand Island. I'd feel much safer with a dog in the house."

"Goliath won't mind staying in the backyard. Maybe Daddy and I can build him a doghouse to sleep in."

"No, he's used to staying inside. Your father and I agree it would be best for all of us if Goliath stayed in the house anytime he wants but especially at night."

Tassie tilted her head in question. "You're not just saying that because you think it will please me?"

Mrs. Springer lifted her hand, witness-style. "Honest, we really do want Goliath inside."

"I had no idea he'd get that big when I got him. He has been terrific company. I don't know what I would have done without him."

"Then it's settled. Goliath comes inside whenever he wants. Come on, let's eat supper. I'm sure your father is already at the table."

Once the three were seated and her father had prayed, he reached across and grasped his daughter's hand. "I can't tell you how happy we are to have you home again. We've missed you."

Tassie swallowed at the emotional lump in her throat. "It's good to be home, Daddy."

Opal Springer picked up the platter of golden pan-fried chicken and handed it to her. "I've fixed your favorites, sweet-heart, even lemon meringue pie for dessert."

"Thanks, Mom. Everything looks wonderful, but you shouldn't have gone to so much trouble." She carefully perused the platter then selected a beautifully browned breast, her favorite piece.

Her father speared a pickled beet with his fork. "Have you decided what kind of job you'd like for the summer?"

"Not really, not that I have such terrific skills to offer an employer. I didn't mind my job at the photo shop but I can't say I'd want to do it again. I'd like to get a job at the hospital or a doctor's office, but I doubt they'd want to hire and train me when I'm only going to be there for three months. I'd have to be honest with them. But I am going to apply at those places anyway. I've also thought about maybe a job as a salesclerk at Dillard's or Penney's in the Conestoga Mall. They usually hire summertime help and I might be able to work for them on weekends after school starts."

"What about one of the Wal-Mart stores? They always seem to be hiring."

"I've thought of that. I guess I'll just start making the rounds tomorrow and see what I can find."

They finished their meal with pleasant conversation and then, after helping her mother clear the table and load the dishwasher, Tassie went to her room to unpack the bags and boxes she'd brought in from her car. Later that night, after giving Goliath's head a final pat, she switched off the lamp and lay snuggled up all cozy in her bed, staring at the luminous stars stuck to her ceiling, the ones she had placed there when she was in junior high, and she felt warm and comfy. At long last, she was home again and it felt oh so good.

❧

Unfortunately, some of that feeling of euphoria disappeared the next morning as she left the hospital and walked from store to store in the mall in search of employment. Three hours later, weary in both mind and body and filled with discouragement, she headed for home.

"How'd it go?" her mom asked as Tassie entered the house and tossed her purse onto the kitchen counter.

"Not good. When the lady at the hospital human relations office discovered I'll be starting college in the fall, the only job she offered me was in food preparation in the hospital kitchen, a minimum wage job with crazy hours. I had hoped for more. No one else where I applied or inquired wanted full-time help, especially for only three short months."

"What about Wal-Mart? Did you go there? They may be interested in summer help."

Tassie kicked off her shoes and wiggled her toes. Her feet hurt. "I'm going there first thing in the morning."

"I'm sure you'll find something, dear. You just have to be patient."

"Patient? I don't have time to be patient. By scrimping, I've managed to save almost enough to enroll in college but not nearly enough to stay there." She lifted her hands in frustration. "No full-time job, no school."

"I've told you your father and I will help."

"Thanks for offering, Mom, but no. I have to do this on my own."

"But. . ."

Tassie lifted her hand. "No, Mom, I mean it. Just letting me stay here at home until I get on my feet is more than enough." She grinned at her mother then bent and kissed her cheek. "Besides, I know you're praying for me. Surely God will answer prayer. Where is your faith?"

By eleven o'clock the next morning, Tassie had already been to Dillard's, Penney's, Wal-Mart, Target, Super Saver, and Skagway, with each manager saying he or she would go over her application then call her, as if all she had to do was wait by the phone. From there she trudged on to Walgreen's, U-Save Foods, Bag 'N Save, and Pump and Pantry, with much the same results, although one of the managers she met with did give her a little hope.

"So how did it go today?" her father asked after the three had gathered around the dinner table and thanked the Lord for their food. "Find anything promising?"

Tassie huffed as she unfolded her napkin and placed it in her lap. "'Promising' isn't exactly the word I would use to describe my day. Grueling would be more like it."

"I take that to mean you didn't have any success."

She felt her mother's hand lovingly circle her forearm. "Perhaps tomorrow will be better, dear."

Tomorrow—how she hated to even think about doing the same thing the next day. "Maybe I made a mistake coming back to Grand Island. Not that living in Omaha was so terrific, but at least there seemed to be more jobs there. But that's hindsight. I've already quit my job and given up my apartment. Don't worry, Mom. God knows I need a job. He won't let me down."

Later, as the two were cleaning the kitchen, her mother received a call on her cell phone from one of her friends at church. Tassie smiled at her then shooed her out of the room, motioning that she would finish the job herself. When the kitchen was finally back to order, she moved into the living room and sat down on the sofa beside her father. "I love you, Daddy," she told him, leaning her head against his shoulder.

He lowered his newspaper and smiled at her. She loved his smile. Why couldn't she have inherited his dimples?

Grinning and excited about something, her mother flitted across the room toward them. "Tassie, guess what! I think I have a job for you!"

Before Tassie could respond, her mother wiggled her way

in between the two and sat down. "That was Phyllis Cramer. She said her neighbor is frantic for a babysitter for his three children!"

None too enthused, Tassie screwed up her face. "Thanks, Mom, but I don't think so. I love children, and have had plenty of experience as a babysitter, but I need a full-time job."

"It is full time, actually more than full time. He wants a live-in nanny, and Phyllis says she thinks the pay is pretty good. She's already highly recommended you!"

She frowned. "Why would a man need a live-in nanny? Where's his wife?"

"Gone. Killed in a car wreck a few years ago I think Phyllis said."

"Doesn't the guy spend any time with his kids?"

"Yes, as much as he can, I guess. She said he needs someone there 24-7 because he works odd hours and is sometimes called out on a case for days."

"Case? What's he do?"

"Oh, I guess I didn't mention that. Phyllis said he is a detective. His wife's mother has been living with him and caring for the children but apparently there was some kind of disagreement and she has moved to California. Phyllis has been pinch-hitting and taking care of them until he finds a replacement. I think you should go see him."

Tassie gave her head a slight shake. "I don't know, Mom. He's probably looking for someone on a permanent basis. I doubt he'd want to hire me for just three months then have to find someone to replace me."

"You've always been great with kids. You ought to at least talk to him, find out exactly what he does want." She reached into her apron pocket and pulled out a piece of notepaper. "My friend gave me his number."

Tassie took it and stuck it into her jeans' pocket. "I'll think about it. Meantime, I'm going to go out in the backyard and toss the Frisbee to Goliath."

❧

As she dressed the next morning in preparation for hitting the pavement again in search of a job, she remembered she had left her car keys in the pocket of her jeans and reached into the closet to retrieve them. As she pulled the keys out, a folded piece of paper fell to the floor. But as she picked it up and turned to toss it onto her dresser she stopped. Maybe she should give that man a call; then at least she could tell her mother she had tried. Most retail stores didn't open until ten so she still had plenty of time before slipping on her shoes and heading out. Pulling her cell phone from her pocket, she dialed the number. To her surprise he answered on the first ring.

"Mr. Drummond? This is Tassie Springer. I've just moved back to town and I'm looking for a job. Phyllis Cramer, a friend of my mother, said you were searching for a full-time babysitter. I thought—"

"When can you come for an interview?"

What? I know Mrs. Cramer recommended me but isn't he going to ask about my qualifications? "I—I guess I could come anytime it is convenient for you."

"Where are you now?"

"Now? At—at my parents' home on Wilson Way Road."

"What's the house number?"

"Ten sixteen, but—"

"I'll be there in ten minutes." A click sounded in her ear.

Still holding the phone in her hand, Tassie staggered her way into the kitchen where her mother was preparing the ingredients to go into the bread machine. "He's coming here."

Her mother screwed the lid onto the bottle of ground cinnamon then swung around. "Who's coming here?"

"The guy who needs a babysitter. Mitchell Drummond."

three

Mitch double-checked the address then punched the door-bell button with one hand and worked at his tie with the other. This woman—this Tassie Springer, if he liked her and felt she would do a good job—had to say yes. *At this point I'd almost settle for an orangutan as a babysitter if it could keep my kids in line.* He smiled to himself. *Maybe that's not such a bad idea. Wonder where I could get one.*

When a lovely late-fortyish-looking woman answered the door, smiling at him, he thought maybe God had heard his prayers after all. "I'm Mitchell Drummond. I'm the one who needs a babysitter—ah, I guess these days they call them a nanny, someone full time." When she pushed open the screen door he quickly stepped inside.

"Would you like a glass of lemonade? I made it fresh not more than an hour ago."

He sat down as she gestured toward the sofa. "Thank you, no." Then glancing around the room and being pleased with what he saw, he offered, "Lovely place you have here. So homey. Have you had much experience taking care of children?"

Her hand went to her throat as she gasped. "Oh, I'm not the one interested in the job. It's my daughter, Tassie. And as for your question, yes, she has had lots of child-care experience. As a teenager, she babysat for several families on a regular basis. Then when she went off to college she babysat for her neighbor's children while the woman worked nights and weekends. She'll be here in a moment, Mr. Drummond. She went outside to spend a few minutes with her dog."

Both he and the woman turned as an attractive young female came hurrying into the room and extended her hand.

"Hi. I'm Tassie Springer. You're Mr. Drummond?"

"Yes." He rose quickly and shook her hand. "Nice to meet you, Miss Springer."

After motioning him to be seated, she sat down across from him as her mother said a hasty good-bye and scurried from the room. "I hope I haven't wasted your time. I never expected you to rush all the way over here before we'd even had a chance to visit on the phone. You never even asked me about my qualifications."

"Your mom took care of that after I got here. She told me about all the babysitting you've done. And you did come highly recommended."

"Oh? Then you know more about me than I know about you. Tell me about this nanny position of yours, your children, and what is expected of whomever you hire."

This woman sounds perfect for the job. "Well, my wife died a couple of years ago and since then, her mother has been living with us, caring for the children and running the house." He nervously cleared his throat. "I have to be honest with you. Actually, my three children have been running her, and the house has pretty much gone unattended. My kids can be a real handful."

"I was sorry to hear about your wife. Her loss must have really been hard on you and your family."

"It has been hard. *But not as hard as the day she walked out on us to go live with her drunken biker boyfriend.* "We have tried to manage, but now that my mother-in-law has moved to California I'm without a babysitter."

"You have three children?"

"Yes, Babette, she's four. Tony, he's thirteen, and Delana, she'll be sixteen soon. After my wife died I used some of the life insurance money to buy a new minivan, so you'll have dependable transportation to drive the children around to their activities. You'll have a room of your own, of course, up above the garage, but I would expect you to sleep in the house on the nights when I have to be away. On the sofa or maybe in one of the girls' rooms."

"And you expect the person you hire to live at your home seven days a week, with no days off? Not even Sundays?"

"Oh, I'm sure I'll be able to spare you at least one day each week, they just won't be regular. I'm a detective, so my schedule is pretty hectic. I may work fifty hours one week and eighty the next. It depends on what's happening on Grand Island's crime scene. I just need to make sure if I'm out all night, or get a phone call and am called away, someone is there with the children."

"Is there anything else you'd like to know about me? I'm sure it must be difficult even thinking about turning your children and your home over to a complete stranger."

"I should probably ask more questions but I can't think of any right now. I'm not very good at this sort of thing, but one thing I am good at is judging people. In my business you get so you can read 'em like a book, and you have had experience with children. Just meeting you and talking with your mother, I can tell you'll work out fine. It's obvious you've come from a pretty nice family."

She gave him a weak smile. "You—ah—haven't mentioned the pay."

"Oh, I haven't, have I?" He rubbed at his chin and gave it some thought. If he made it too low, she would probably say no without even considering it. And taking care of his kids wasn't going to be any picnic. He threw out a figure he hoped would seem fair. "And, of course, other than your personal items, I'll pay all your expenses while you're there."

He watched while she gave it some thought, hoping and praying she would say yes. He was prepared to go a bit higher in wages if he had to, but not much. He made a decent salary with the Grand Island Police Department but it was never enough to do everything he would like to do for his family. "Well, what's your answer?"

Tassie scrunched up her face in thought. "I'll admit I wasn't too interested in the job when I first heard about it, mainly because I'd be working so many hours, but I could really use the salary you're offering, Mr. Drummond. I've always liked and gotten along well with kids, so I'm not concerned about that part. And, thanks to my mom, I know how to clean. And when I was living at home she turned me into a pretty good cook—but there may be a problem we haven't yet discussed. A problem I would have mentioned on the phone if you'd given me half a chance."

He leaned forward with a reassuring smile, willing to do whatever it took to get her to say yes. "I'm sure we can overcome whatever it is." The more she said, the better he liked her. He had to convince her to accept his offer.

"You said you needed someone full time. Working full time would be fine for me now, but I can only work through the summer. I'm going to go back to college in the fall. I want to get my degree."

Mitch felt as if he had been kicked in the stomach. Tassie had seemed so right for the job. Finding a nanny—one who would live in—was proving to be far more difficult than he had imagined when his mother-in-law just up and walked out on him without notice. "Only through the summer?"

"Yes. I'm sorry but I had to be honest with you. Since that apparently won't work out for you, I do hope you can find someone else. I know how concerned you must be, being without proper child care, especially since your children will soon be out of school for summer break. Couldn't Delana care for her brother and sister until the fall semester begins? You said she was almost sixteen. I started babysitting when I was only twelve."

"Actually, I prefer to have an adult with them." *As disobedient as Delana is, there is no way that would work out. She would have the house filled with her friends the minute I left for work.* He shuddered. *Friends or boyfriends!* Filled with disappointment, he rose and headed toward the door. "You sure I can't change your mind?"

"No, I dropped out of college once and I'm not going to let that happen again. I'm determined to get my degree."

He opened the door then stepped outside. "Keep my number just in case, okay?"

"I will but I won't be changing my mind. Nice to have met you, Mr. Drummond. I wish you the best."

When the door closed behind him, he stood on the porch for a moment, half tempted to ring the doorbell again and beg her to take the job. She had seemed so right. But he didn't. She had said no and he had to accept it. Finishing college and getting her degree was important to her and certainly admirable. It wasn't fair to even tempt her to give up such a noble thing.

But as he climbed into his car and headed for the police station, he couldn't help but compare the excitement he had felt on the way to Tassie's house to how he felt now. Lousy.

❧

Tassie received calls from two prospective employers the next day with each offering no more than minimum wage and less than twenty-five hours per week. As much as she hated to, she turned them down. She filled out applications at several more of the smaller shops in the mall then headed home, discouraged and again second-guessing her move back to

Grand Island. Was this God's way of punishing her? Wasn't living with what she had done all those years ago punishment enough? Did He have to heap on more?

"What's wrong, sweetheart?" her father asked that evening. "Your mom told me about the nanny job you turned down. Is that what's upsetting you?"

She sat down next to him and snuggled close. He felt warm, safe, just like he had when she had been a child and had snuggled up to him with a book in her hand, hoping he would read her a story. "Sorta, I guess, that and being rejected by all the places where I've applied for jobs. I feel so low, Dad, like I'm of no value to anyone."

"You are to me, honey, and to your mom. Next to our Lord and each other, we love you more than any person on earth."

"I know, Daddy, and I love you for loving me, but I'm a twenty-six-year-old woman now. Not a child. I should be able to make it on my own. I can't come running to you and Mom all my life."

"We like having you run to us; we just wish we could do more. God knows your needs, Tassie."

"I know, but my need right now is a job, and so far He hasn't given me one."

Off in the distance a phone rang. Tassie leaped to her feet. "Be right back; that's my cell phone. I left it in my room." She hurried down the hall, hoping to get there before her voice mail picked up or the person hung up. "Hello," she answered breathlessly.

"Miss Springer?" said a familiar voice.

"Yes?"

"Hi, Tassie. This is Mitch. Mitch Drummond."

"Oh?" Disappointed it wasn't another job offer, she felt her hopes deflate. "I'm really sorry, Mr. Drummond. I know you need a nanny but I can't change my mind. I *am* going to college in the fall."

"What if I told you I wanted you to work only *until* the fall semester?"

Slightly heartened, Tassie switched the phone to her other ear and sat down on the edge of her bed. "I—I don't understand."

"Look, I need a nanny, babysitter, or whatever you want to call it, and I need one now. You're available now, but only until the fall semester begins. Finding the right person for this job is proving to be much harder than I had anticipated and you seemed so right for it. So I got to thinking. *If* you agree to take the job only until your classes start, that will give me slightly over three months to find your replacement. Surely in that length of time I can find someone competent. It's a win-win situation for both of us. What do you say?"

She hurriedly thought over his offer. He was right, it would be a win-win situation for both of them and she could sure use the kind of money he had offered. "Going to church is important to me. I'd have to have Sundays off." *Lord, if You want me to accept this job, please work things out so I won't have to miss church.*

From the pause on the other end she figured she had blown it, that he wouldn't agree since he had been so adamant about her working a flexible schedule; but that's the way it had to be. He could take it or leave it.

"Having *every* Sunday off might present a problem. The bad guys don't take Sundays off. Crime happens seven days a week and when it occurs I need to be there."

As much as she wanted to take the job, she couldn't. She had to honor God and stand her ground. "Then I'm sorry, really I am, but attending church is important to me."

When he paused again and the connection lay heavy with silence, she thought he had hung up on her. But as she pulled the phone from her ear and started to flip it closed, he said, "I have an idea that may work for both of us, if you're agreeable to it."

Please, Lord, don't let him offer me more money if I work Sundays. I don't want to be tempted to miss church.

"You could take my kids with you."

"To church?" His suggestion was one she should have thought of herself and she almost felt ashamed for not offering to take them. "I'd love to have your children go to church with me." *Thank You, God!*

"I'm afraid I haven't been a very good father. I used to attend but I haven't taken them since my wife—ah—died, and my mother-in-law certainly never took them. I like the idea of my children attending church."

"What if they wouldn't want to go with me?"

"They may rebel at first but I'm sure they'll come around once they get used to it. I might even come with you, too, on the Sundays I don't have to work. Believe it or not, I used to be pretty active in our church, even sang in the choir for a year or two. So will you come to work for me? I'd like you to start as soon as possible."

"Like—how soon?"

"Tomorrow?"

"And you'll pay me what you originally offered?"

"Absolutely, and if things go as well as I hope they will, there may be a small severance bonus for you when your classes start."

The job seemed to be everything she had hoped for and more. "I accept, Mr. Drummond. I'll gather up my things and report to your home in the morning no later than eight o'clock."

"Could you possibly make it by seven? I want to introduce you to my children before the two older ones leave for school, and I have to be at the courthouse by eight."

She glanced at her watch. Seven was less than thirteen hours away. She'd have to pack, load her car, take a shower—

"But if seven is a problem, I could—"

"Seven will be fine, Mr. Drummond. I'll see you in the morning."

Another thought occurred to her, an important one. "Oh, I have another problem, one I haven't mentioned. I have a dog. I can't leave Goliath here and expect my parents to take care of him."

"Goliath? He's not a Great Dane, is he?"

She chuckled. "No, but he's a big dog. A black Lab."

A sigh of relief sounded on the other end. "Bring him. My backyard is fenced in and my son has always wanted a dog. Besides, I've heard black Labs make great family pets."

"They do."

"Is he an outdoor dog or used to staying in the house?"

"He stayed in my apartment most of the time when I was in Omaha but—"

"Don't worry about it. He can stay in the house if he wants. I'm sure my kids will like him."

"That's very kind of you, Mr. Drummond."

"Then I'll see you—and Goliath—at seven. The address is—"

"Just a moment, let me get a pen," she said as she grabbed a pen and paper from her nightstand. "Okay, I'm ready."

"It's 2442 East Windmill Lane. It's the only quad-level in the block. My red car will be parked in the driveway."

"I'm sure I can find it. I'll see you at seven."

❧

Early the next morning, Mitch glanced at the clock on the range, gulped down the final swig of coffee, then hurried to the bottom of the steps leading to the upstairs bedrooms. "Tony! Delana! I need you downstairs now. We need to talk.

Your new nanny will be here in fifteen minutes," he hollered, cupping his hands to his mouth.

No response.

He brought his hands together in a loud clap. "Delana, Tony. Did you hear me? I said now. It's six forty-five. You need to at least eat a bowl of cereal before leaving for school."

Still no response.

"Am I going to have to come up there and get you? Because if I do, I'll guarantee you it won't be pleasant. Come down here right now! That's an order."

The only sound in response was the loud slamming of a door.

Mitch grabbed the handrail and, taking two steps at a time, rushed up to the landing. "Last call. I mean it. I want both of you out here right now!"

The bathroom door opened and Tony, sending his father a look of disgust, emerged in a pair of baggy jeans, his underwear sticking out over the top, and a shirt with the words SCHOOL IS FOR IDIOTS AND LOSERS emblazoned across the front, his hair in a feeble attempt at a spiked-up Mohawk.

"Quit yer dreamin', Dad. That woman won't last a day."

Mitch wanted to grab his son, order him to get rid of the weird hairdo, and shove him back into the bathroom, but he didn't. The last thing he needed was a scene when Tassie arrived. "She'd better last more than a day or you'll have me to answer to. I expect the three of you to be on your best behavior."

With a snort Tony pushed his way past Mitch and headed downstairs to the kitchen. Mitch walked the few steps to Delana's door and rapped softly. "Delana, come on out, sweetheart. It's nearly time for Tassie to arrive."

When Delana didn't respond, Mitch turned the knob and, knowing how angry his daughter got when he invaded her privacy, pushed the door open only a slight crack. "Honey, did you hear Daddy?"

When she didn't answer, he pushed the door fully open and stepped inside. To his dismay the room was empty. Mitch's heart sank as he saw the open window. He hurriedly walked over and closed it, making sure to hook the latch. If his daughter had climbed out the window, as she had done several times before to spend the night with one of her girlfriends, when she came back home she'd have to come through the door. But what was he going to tell Tassie? If he told her the truth, that his daughter was nothing more than a rebel teenager who constantly disobeyed his orders, she'd probably walk out and he'd be back to square one—without a nanny.

Struggling to set his anger over Delana aside he moved down the hall and, ignoring the KEEP OUT sign his four-year-old had taped to her door, he turned the knob, entered her room, bent over the sleeping child, and gently placed a loving kiss on her pink cheek.

Without even opening her eyes, Babette pushed him away. "Leave me alone!"

"Daddy was just trying to wake you up, baby. Your new babysitter will be here. . ."

He stopped mid-sentence at the ringing of the doorbell. *Oh, no. She's early!* "Get your clothes on, pumpkin then come downstairs, okay?"

Babette flipped onto her side and yanked the covers over her head. "Don't want to."

"Please. For Daddy?"

The doorbell sounded a second time. Mitch swallowed hard then went to answer it.

❧

Tassie stepped back from the door and surveyed her surroundings. The house was nice. Well-painted and, except for two pairs of muddy running shoes and an equally muddy skateboard lying on the porch, it was fairly neat. The grass had been recently mowed but not edged, and the flower beds boasted no flowers, only weeds, but Mitchell Drummond was a single, apparently overworked father. More than likely, planting flowers and making sure his lawn was edged wasn't in the top ten on his priority list. She pressed the button again and waited. Finally, the door opened and Mr. Drummond's smiling face appeared.

"Sorry, I was—my daughter Babette and I were—ah—talking." He motioned her inside.

She nodded then stepped into the foyer, which was nothing more than a closet door on one side and on the other, a chest with a mirror—desperately in need of a good washing—above it. She followed him into the living room.

"The kids are—ah—getting ready for school. Well, Tony is, or was, now he's in the kitchen having breakfast." His gaze went to the stairway, which was directly behind the sofa. "Since Babette is only four, she doesn't go to school. She's—ah—sleeping. I'm sure she'll wake up in a little while." He gestured toward the stairway. "The kids' bedrooms are upstairs. They share the hall bathroom." He pointed to a set of stairs leading to a lower level. "A second bathroom is down there and so is the family room. It has a fireplace. My bedroom is in the lowest level."

Tassie nodded. "What about the laundry room?"

He pointed toward an archway on his left. "By the back door."

"No dining room?"

"Not really, but the kitchen has space for an oblong table and six chairs."

"And I'm to sleep above the garage?"

"Yes. Sorry about the inconvenience. The stairway to the

garage room is on the outside. But," he hastened to add, "there is an intercom so when I have to leave during the night, I'll be able wake you up without coming to your room. I'd show it to you now but I want you to meet Tony before his ride comes to pick him up."

"Before I do anything, I need to get Goliath out of my car."

"Oh, yes, Goliath. I nearly forgot about him." Mr. Drummond took the small suitcase from her hand and placed it on the floor. But as he reached for the doorknob the front door opened and a teenage girl, her hair a tangled mess, mascara smeared on her upper cheeks, wearing too-red lipstick and long earrings that dangled precariously to her slim shoulders, entered.

Tassie took one look at the girl's belligerent expression as she glared at her father, then at the teen's skimpy attire, and shuddered. Surely this wasn't Delana—but deep down inside she knew it was. And if it was, and Tony was even half as rebellious as his sister appeared to be, Tassie's work was cut out for her. She could hardly wait to meet Babette. Surely, being only four, she wouldn't yet have had a chance to be tainted by the world—and her siblings.

From the way Mitchell's face reddened and the way he clenched his fists at his sides, Tassie knew the girl was in trouble. "Go wash all that stuff off your face," he told her in an almost monotone. Although Tassie couldn't see his face, she was sure he was gritting his teeth. "I'll deal with you later, Delana. I have to be at the courthouse by eight."

Without a word, Delana gave him a flip of her shoulders and headed up the stairs.

"Better hurry!" he called up after her. "Your friend's mom will be here any minute to take you to school and I want you to meet Tassie." Mitchell raised his brow and gave Tassie a sheepish grin. "That girl has no sense of time."

Tassie felt her eyes widen. How dumb did he think she was? It was obvious the girl had been out all night! Hadn't he been aware she'd been gone?

Both she and Mitchell turned as Tony waddled into the room. Tassie had never been able to figure out why a guy would want to wear pants hung so low they impeded his walking. And his hair! What a mess.

"Hey, is somebody going to drive me to school? I think my ride forgot to pick me up."

"Drive you to school? No, it's only a couple of blocks away. Walk. The walk will be good for you."

Trying to be friendly, Tassie sent Tony a smile. "Hi. You must be Tony. I'm Tassie. I'll walk out with you. I want to introduce you to Goliath."

The boy wrinkled up his nose. "Who is Goliath?"

Tassie crooked her finger in his direction. "Come with me and I'll show you."

Without even a good-bye to his dad, Tony followed her as she walked out the front door toward her car.

"Wow! Goliath is a dog!"

The smile on his face warmed Tassie's heart. Every boy she had ever known had been crazy about dogs. Maybe Goliath would be the very thing she needed to establish some sort of common ground with Tony. "You like dogs?"

He reached inside and stroked Goliath's head. "Yeah, I always wanted a dog, but Dad said no." Then turning to her he asked, "Is he going to let you keep him here? In the house?"

"Yes, he said it was fine with him."

Tony reared back, his eyes rounded. "*My* dad said that?"

"Sure did." She pointed toward Goliath. "He likes you. I can tell."

"I like him, too. Wow, Dad said a dog could stay here. Wait'll I tell Delana. She'll never believe it. He must have been pretty desperate for a babysitter to hire one with a dog."

"Your big sister likes dogs?"

Tony cautiously leaned into the open door. "Yeah. She kept one of those fancy little dogs in her closet for three days before my dad found out. Boy, did she get in trouble for that one."

"You think she'll like Goliath? He's a lot bigger than one of those fancy little dogs."

The boy stroked the dog's ears. "Yeah, she'll like him. Who wouldn't? He's a great dog. Babette'll like him, too."

Tassie suddenly felt a warm burst of satisfaction. Thanks to Goliath, maybe living with the Drummond kids wouldn't be so bad after all; but of course she still hadn't yet met the third child. She'd have to wait and see what Babette was like.

At only four years old, she couldn't be too bad. Could she?

four

After a few final words with Mr. Drummond, he unceremoniously handed her a house key as he headed out the door, Delana on his heels, ignoring Tassie's good-bye as the girl rushed out to meet her ride. She closed and locked the front door. Then, after checking to make sure Babette was still asleep, Tassie made a second trip out to her car, filled her arms with a few of the remaining items, then led Goliath back into the house.

"The situation here is a little different than at Mom and Dad's," she told him as the two moved through the house and up the outside stairway to her room.

"Um, not bad," she said aloud after glancing round the small room that was to be hers for the next three months. "You and I are going to have to be patient. I have a feeling these kids are going to try to walk all over us." Once everything had been placed on her bed or on the floor for sorting out later, Tassie, leaving Goliath behind, moved back downstairs to check on Babette and establish her presence in the Drummond home. If she demonstrated her authority right from the beginning, perhaps the children would be more cooperative. Even though she would do it in a pleasant manner, she would let them know right up front what she expected of them.

Ignoring the KEEP OUT sign, although just the sight of it infuriated her that a four-year-old child could have such dominion over a household, Tassie tapped on Babette's door. "Hi, Babette. It's me—Tassie. Are you awake? Can I come in?"

"No! Stay out! This is my room!" came back the answer. "I don't like you and I don't want you here!"

The voice was that of a near baby but the words definitely conveyed her meaning. Little Miss Babette wasn't about to accept the newest addition to her home. Turning, Tassie hurried through the house and up the stairs to her room to get Goliath. "Come on, Goliath, I've got a job for you."

With the dog at her heels, she climbed down the outside stairway and back through the house to the bedroom wing. "Someone wants to meet you, Babette. Come and see who it is."

"Don't want to. Go away."

Tassie gave Goliath's head a pat. "I think you're going to like this new friend." Although it took a great deal of effort on her part, she tried to keep her words sweet and not show the impatience that was building inside her.

No response. She pushed the door open a little farther and stuck her head inside, only to be pelted by a flying pink flip-flop. Her impatience turned to anger. Holding her hands in front of her face to ward off any other objects that might come flying her way, she pushed the door fully open and entered the room. There, standing on the bed in the middle of a jumbled combination of dirty clothes and rumpled sheets, stood the young girl, still in her cute little Barbie jammies, her hands on her hips, her chin jutted out defiantly. "Get out!"

Undaunted, Tassie grabbed Goliath's collar and tugged him toward her. "See, I told you someone wanted to meet you. This is Goliath. He's going to be living with you this summer."

"Don't like dogs!"

"But Goliath is such a nice dog. He wants to be your friend."

Babette stomped her little foot, pointed a finger toward the door, and screamed at the top of her lungs, "I hate you! Get out!"

Tassie edged closer. "Now you know that's not true, Babette. You don't even know me, so how can you hate me? I want to be your friend, too."

Babette leaped off the bed, barely landing on her feet, and grabbed a cell phone from her nightstand. "My daddy is a policeman. I'm going to call and tell him to take you to jail!"

The child had her own cell phone? Tassie could only imagine what would happen if Babette did call 911 and told them some awful tale, which she wouldn't put past the belligerent child. Struggling to keep her voice even, she moved quickly forward and took the phone from the little girl's hand. "You don't really want to call the police. Besides, your daddy wants me here. Wouldn't you rather pet Goliath's head? He wants someone to play ball with him."

Babette narrowed her eyes, then folding her arms across her slim chest, glared at Tassie. "Don't want to play ball."

"Then how about coming downstairs and letting me fix you some breakfast? Maybe some nicely browned bacon and French toast? Do you like French toast? With maple syrup on it?"

The child's lower lip curled down. "Don't want no breakfast."

It was obvious she wasn't getting anywhere with the stubborn little girl. "Well, Goliath and I are hungry. I guess, since you don't want any breakfast, I'll go downstairs and fix bacon and French toast for the two of us. If you change your mind, come on down."

As promised, Tassie fixed the bacon and French toast in hopes Babette would relent and join them, but by the time she had finished the plateful she had made for herself, Babette still hadn't appeared on the scene.

"What do I do now?" Tassie asked her mom in desperation after she had dialed her number and described Mr. Drummond's children's behavior. "I've never seen such rebellious children."

"The best thing you can do: Pray for them, ask God for wisdom and strength, and be a shining witness to them."

"Thanks, Mom. You always know the right words to say. From now on, I'm going to look at my position here as a ministry, the ministry God has called me to. But please pray He will make me love these children because, to be honest, they are not very lovable."

"You know I will. Just remember each time they're giving you fits, you're not alone; I'm praying for you *and* for them. Hang in there, sweetheart. Things are bound to get better once they know you. Just love them, Tassie. That's all God requires of you."

With her mother's encouraging words ringing in her ears like a melodious sonnet, Tassie set about cleaning the kitchen and sorting the clothing and other soiled items that had accumulated on the laundry room floor. After that she worked at running the sweeper and dusting everything on the main level. Next, she moved upstairs, deciding first to work on Tony's room.

Until she opened the door and stepped inside.

The place was a shambles with the bedding half pulled off the bed onto the floor. Underwear, T-shirts, and socks were scattered everywhere. There were even drink glasses and ice cream bowls with mold growing in them, green as grass. The room smelled bad. Determined to get it organized, and with plans of making sure it stayed that way, she dove into the mess with a vengeance.

"Tony is going to be mad at you."

Tassie spun around to find Babette standing in the open door, a ragged teddy bear cuddled in her arms, and she was still dressed in her jammies. And on the front of her shirt was a stain—a stain that looked remarkably like maple syrup. Had the child slipped downstairs and enjoyed breakfast while

Tassie was cleaning her brother's room? Ignoring the stain, she continued working.

"Tony may not like it when he realizes I've been in his room, but I'll bet he'll be glad to find everything put away and his bed made. Most boys don't like to make their bed."

"I'm going to tell my daddy you were in Tony's room."

"You can tell him if you like. He hired me to take care of his family. Cooking, doing laundry, and cleaning are part of that job. I have a feeling your father, too, will be glad I did it." Then making sure her smile was pleasant and friendly, she added, "I was going to work on your sister's room next but I can do yours first, if you like."

Babette's face took on a scowl. "No! Don't want you in my room. Stay out!"

Tassie watched as the girl darted out of the room then flinched when she heard Babette's door slam. That little girl was going to be a real challenge, but she'd be patient, just like her mother had said she should; and hopefully, by the time her three-plus months were up, they'd all be friends.

She was still standing in the middle of the room, trying to figure out her next step, when the phone rang. It was Mr. Drummond, checking to see how things were going. Deciding she really hadn't been on the job long enough to honestly evaluate the situation, she dodged his question by turning the tables and asking how his day was going.

"Not too great," he answered with a heavy sigh. "This case we're working on really has me baffled. Looks like I won't make it home for supper like I'd planned, maybe not even until morning. I might be involved in an important all-night stakeout. I hate it that this is happening on your first day. Is everything going okay with Babette?"

"I—think so."

"Good. You have the number. Remember, you can always call

me on my cell phone if you have questions or any problems."

"Thank you. I will. You have a good day," she told him before cutting the connection.

"Well," she told Goliath as she hung up the phone, "Mr. Drummond isn't going to make it home for supper. That means I'll be dealing with his children by myself tonight. I was hoping he'd be here to help get things off to a good start, but that isn't going to happen."

Goliath met her words with a cock of his head.

"And if he is involved in that stakeout I'll be spending my first night on the sofa instead of the bed in my room." She smiled at the dog. "Guess where you'll be sleeping. On the floor right next to me."

At noon Tassie fixed two peanut butter and lettuce sandwiches. One she ate, the other she placed on a plate on a pretty placemat and added carrot and celery sticks, in hopes that Babette would come into the kitchen when she wasn't looking and eat like she had done with her breakfast plate. By one o'clock, the sandwich lay exactly where she had placed it. But the next time she passed through the kitchen the plate was empty.

After checking the refrigerator to make sure she had everything she would need to prepare supper, she made her way back upstairs to Delana's room to work on the trash that was strewn all over the furniture and carpet. How anyone could live in such filth and enjoy it was beyond her.

Like most young girls, she herself had been rebellious as a teenager, but even with that she had kept her room in fairly decent order. Not as neat as her mother would have preferred, but decent. Not Delana's. Her room was knee-deep with discarded clothing, hats, purses, scarves, shoes, hair clips, perfume bottles, shopping bags, empty hair spray cans, wadded up paper, fast-food wrappers and Styrofoam containers, napkins, and drinking straws. There were also textbooks, spiral notebooks, jewel cases from both computer software and music CDs, discarded posters, numerous partially used bottles of nail polish, playbills, receipts—you name it and it was probably there. Tassie stood in the middle of the muddle staring at it. The job looked impossible. She hardly knew where to begin.

"*What* are you doing in my room?" a stern voice asked from behind her.

She turned and found two dark-rimmed eyes glaring at her from beneath heavily darkened eyebrows and a head of hair boasting a broad streak of green running through her bangs. It wasn't time for school to be out. Had this girl actually gone to school or had she skipped classes? Maybe spent the day with friends? She hadn't had that streak of green when she'd left the house this morning.

"I'm cleaning your room but now that you're here you can help me," she answered, forcing a smile and trying to sound nonchalant.

"I don't want my room cleaned. I liked it the way it was. You have no right to be in here." The girl pointed a long fake nail painted with shiny black polish toward the door. "Get out!"

"Look, Delana, I know life hasn't been easy for you. Your father hired me to take care of you and your brother and sister because he loves you and is concerned about you. All I'm doing is making sure the trash is sorted from your personal belongings, throwing it away, and placing your clothing and shoes in their proper places. If you want to finish the job yourself, that's fine with me. I'll even help if you'll let me, but you have to stop throwing everything on the floor. Believe it or not, I was your age once myself and not so long ago. I liked my privacy, too, and my mother let me have it—so long as I did my part and kept my room halfway neat and orderly. That's all I'm asking of you."

Delana's fists went to her hips. "Who do you think you are? God?"

"Of course not, but I did pray about coming here before I took the job."

The girl glared at her. "And you think because you prayed you can come into our home and upset it like this?"

Tassie's eyes scanned the cluttered room.

"This is my space, not yours," Delana snarled. "You have no right to order me around. I'm going to call my dad!"

Giving her a gentle smile, Tassie pulled her cell phone from the side pocket of her jeans and held it out toward the girl. "Here, you can use my phone. I've already put his number on speed dial."

Delana let out a snort, then, ignoring the phone, threw herself onto the bed and kicked off her shoes, letting them thud to the floor. Without another word, Tassie gathered up an armload of the strewn clothing and shoes and placed them in the trash container.

Delana quickly sat straight up, her eyes bugging wide open, her face red and distorted with anger. "How dare you put my things in the wastebasket! I've had those shoes barely a week and that shirt was practically new! I'm going to tell my dad to fire you!"

Tassie picked up several more items and added them to the trash container. "I just supposed since they were on the floor they were trash." She picked up the container and headed toward the door. "If you don't want your precious things thrown away, it might be a good idea to put them where they belong. Because anything I find on the floor I will assume is trash, and it will end up in the Dumpster." She paused in the doorway. "Oh, and I want to remind you, supper will be ready at six."

A heavy object of some sort hit the door as Tassie closed

it behind her and she sucked in a deep breath. *Whew, that was close. This tough love thing is even harder than I imagined it would be, and I still have Tony to contend with when he gets home. I just hope Mr. Drummond will go along with me. Because if he doesn't, and if he can't understand that my heart is in the right place and I'm doing my best to help his kids, I may be quitting this job before my second day even gets here.*

But things didn't go any better. In fact, they got worse. When she walked into the kitchen to prepare the taco salad she had planned to serve for supper, the room looked vandalized. Cupboard doors were standing open with grape jelly smeared on both the doors and the brass handles. More jelly was smeared across the countertops, with at least half the slices from a loaf of bread scattered haphazardly on the table and floor. The refrigerator door was standing open, and on the floor was an overturned carton with the full half-gallon of milk running in a trail across the floor. And, if that wasn't enough, two ice cream cartons lay open and melting on the table.

Tassie wanted to cry. Tony! It had to be Tony who had done this horrible thing while she was upstairs with Delana, but why? Had he come home early too? Surely me expecting him to keep his room clean wasn't enough to cause him to do such a violent, destructive act. But when she discovered the words GO HOME spelled out in red lipstick on the tile above the sink, she knew Tony hadn't done it alone. He'd had an accomplice. A green-streak in her hair accomplice who had probably added her touch before coming upstairs and going into a tirade. It was obvious those kids were trying to get her to leave.

She did the best she could to clean up the mess; after that, she prepared the taco salad. When the children showed up at the supper table, she wanted to personally strangle them with her bare hands, but instead she went through the entire meal without even mentioning the damage they had done to her clean kitchen. Since this was probably the last supper they would be having together, she decided to fake her way through the evening and leave them with a good taste in their mouths. Either that or they'd think her a bigger fool than ever for not wanting to retaliate. But regardless of what they thought, this would be her first and final evening in this house. She was going to quit. Maybe she had misunderstood when she thought God had called her to this family as a ministry. There were plenty of other places she could serve to honor Him, places where her efforts would be appreciated.

By the time their father phoned at nine o'clock to say he wasn't going to make it home until morning because he definitely was going to do the all-night stakeout, not only was Tassie ready to give her notice that she was leaving the next day, but she had begun to pack up the few things she had unpacked.

"I'm really sorry about this, Tassie. Knowing firsthand how uncooperative my children can be, I had hoped to be there early this evening to relieve you, definitely before the children went to bed, but this case I'm working on really has me stymied. It's about a missing child and this is the first real lead I've had. I could ask one of the other guys to fill in for me, but I really want to be there myself in case anything goes down. The guy we're after is a real sleazeball. We have to get him off the streets before he harms another child."

"I—"

"I—I really hope you don't mind having to spend your first night sleeping on the sofa or in one of the girls' rooms," he went on, not giving her a chance to interrupt. "I'd sure like to be sleeping in my own bed tonight. This has been a really rough day. I'm beat, but I need to be here. Maybe I can catch a couple hours' sleep tomorrow."

"But, Mr. Drummond, I—"

"Call me Mitch. Everyone does. I can't tell you how relieved I am to know that both you and your dog are there. I worry about my kids. I want them to grow into loving, responsible adults, so I'm glad you'll be taking them to church with you. I'm definitely planning to go along myself the next time I can wangle a Sunday off." He paused. "Oh, I'm sorry, you started to say something and I interrupted you."

Tassie blew out her cheeks in frustration. From the sound of it, he'd had a really rough day, too, maybe even rougher than hers, and he was going to have to stay awake all night. How could she add to his troubles by announcing that she was quitting and moving out the first thing in the morning?

"You already have too much to think about. We can discuss it tomorrow."

"How did your day go with Tony and Delana? Did they give you any more grief?"

Tassie huffed inwardly. *Mr. Drummond, you don't know the half of it. If what I saw today was their best behavior, I'd never want to be around to witness their worst!* Deciding whatever complaining about the day's happenings could wait until morning, she dodged the question as best she could. "I think you'd better ask Delana, Tony, and Babette. Their take on things might be a little different than mine."

"Hang on a sec."

She could hear mumbling, like he was talking to someone with his hand over the mouthpiece.

"Sorry, my partner is ready to leave. Gotta go. I'll be home sometime in the morning to try to catch a little shut-eye. We'll talk more then. But, Tassie, I want you to know how much I appreciate all you're doing for my family. Thank you for being there."

She swallowed hard. "I—I'll see you in the morning, Mr.—Mitch. Stay safe."

"Stay safe?" He chuckled. "No one has told me that since my mom passed away. She always worried about me. It's nice to hear those words again. You stay safe, too. Good night."

"Good night."

Although Mitch had said he would be home in the morning and he did phone twice the next day, it was nearly six o'clock before he walked through the front door, face drawn, shoulders slumped, and in clothing that looked as if he had spent the night in the car, which he said he had. Tassie had never seen a man look so beat.

She was tired, too—dead tired—from the day spent running the sweeper in rooms that looked as if they hadn't been swept in months, washing windows both inside and out, cleaning bathtubs and showers until they sparkled, and completing a myriad of other household tasks that should have been done on a regular basis. Had Mitch and his children gotten so used to living in such disarray they hadn't even noticed how bad things had become? The only decent and organized room in the house was Mitch's room, and even that had needed a good dusting. She had decided early that morning, since she was going to quit, she was going to leave things in the best possible condition. Maybe that way, whoever replaced her could at least start out with a clean house.

Mitch placed his briefcase on the hall closet floor then dragged himself into the living room. "Wow! Sure looks nice in here. Where'd you put all the stuff?"

She smiled. "In the closets and desk drawers where it belonged."

"Where are the kids?"

She motioned toward the stairs. "Delana and Tony are *supposed* to be in their rooms, doing their homework. Babette is watching a VeggieTales video and playing with her teddy bear."

"VeggieTales?"

"It's a terrific animated series designed for kids, fun for them to watch but with a great message. I picked up the DVD at the Christian bookstore today when I talked Babette into going with me. I bought her a book, too, and she actually let me read it to her."

"That's terrific." His brows rose. "And the other two are doing their homework? That's a first."

"I said *supposed* to be doing their homework. At least they were the last time I looked in on them."

Mitch wandered into the kitchen, Tassie following, and sat down before leaning his elbows on the table and cupping his face in his hands. "Thanks for taking this job, Tassie. I know it's not easy. My kids are a handful. Even though you haven't said much about it, I'm sure they have given you all kinds of trouble both yesterday *and* today. I don't know how to thank you for putting up with them."

"Your children *are* a handful, Mr. Drummond." Somehow, since she was going to complain about his children, it seemed improper to call him by his first name. "I wanted to tell you this yesterday but when you called and said you wouldn't be home at all last night, you had sounded so frustrated and tired that I decided to wait until now. I worked all day yesterday at getting Tony's, Delana's, and Babette's rooms in order, and today at giving the rest of the house a good cleaning. Each of your children's rooms was an absolute catastrophe."

Mitch hung his head. "I know. I'm sorry you had to see them that way. I never expected you to clean them up for them. Cleaning those rooms should be their responsibility."

"You're right. That should be their responsibility but I didn't mind cleaning them. In fact, I had hoped that by seeing them clean they would want to keep them that way. But apparently it didn't work."

"I guess that means things didn't go so well."

"Not well at all. My first real episode yesterday was with Babette and the second with Delana when she came home and found me cleaning her room. After that was with Tony, when he came home from school and saw what I had done to his room. I had half expected your older children to explode when they found I had been in their rooms, but Tony called me names I wouldn't want to repeat. Delana didn't call me names but she made it pretty clear she didn't want me in her room. So did Babette. I was shocked when a four-year-old actually ordered me out of her room and threatened to call the police! I'm sorry to say it because I don't want to hurt you, but your children's behavior has been deplorable. And I haven't even told you about the horrible mess Tony and Delana deliberately made of my clean kitchen by smearing the cabinets, countertops, and floor with grape jelly. Not to mention leaving cartons of ice cream out to melt, the refrigerator door standing open, and a milk carton turned on its side, spilling milk onto the floor I had just mopped."

Mitch gave his head a sad shake. "I'm sorry, Tassie. I don't know what else to say. No one deserves to be treated that way."

"After the day I'd had with them, despite my resolve to stay, I came to the conclusion it might be better if I moved on, looked for another job, and forgot all about your family. But being an old softie, and feeling sorry for running out on you without notice, when all three children showed up for dinner right at six o'clock last night and consumed every bite of the taco salad I had fixed, and you weren't able to make it home all night, I decided I would give things another day, hoping to see improvement. But I wasn't staying today for them, Mr. Drummond, I was staying for you. Unfortunately, I'm sorry to say, today hasn't been any better."

He gazed at her with tired eyes. "I wish I could say I'm surprised by their abhorrent behavior but I'm not. The decent thing would have been to have given you more of a warning before you took the job but I couldn't. I was desperate for someone to stay with them and at my wits' end. As much as I had hoped you'd stay I can't blame you wanting to quit."

"My heart goes out to you because I know you love those kids and want the very best for them, but unfortunately, your children don't think I'm the best. They see me as an enemy."

"They treat everyone as their enemy—me included—and I have no idea what to do about it. I've tried everything from grounding them to taking away their allowance. I've even taken them to a psychiatrist. Nothing works." He shrugged. "I'll pay you for the entire week and I'm sure that doesn't begin to be enough, considering all they have put you through."

"No, I can't let you do that. All I expect to be paid for is the two days I've been here. Of course, since I'll be leaving first thing in the morning, you'll have to make some kind of arrangements for Babette."

"I'll call our neighbor. She won't be too happy about it but after a little persuasion I'm sure she'll agree to help me out again, at least for a day or two."

"Then I guess I'll say good night."

"Yeah, good night. Thanks again, Tassie. You're a terrific person. I wish you only the best."

"Thanks, Mi—Mr. Drummond. I wish things could have worked out differently."

His heavy sigh broke her heart.

"Me, too, Tassie. Me, too."

❧

It was nearly ten o'clock by the time Tassie finished her daily Bible reading and enjoyed a long, hot, relaxing shower. But as she turned off her hair dryer and slipped it into her overnight bag, she remembered she had forgotten to start the dishwasher after loading it with the supper dishes. She would need the stainless steel frying pan to cook the bacon she planned to prepare for breakfast before leaving the next morning.

Quickly pulling on her robe over her pajamas, she made her way down the outside stairs and into the kitchen. But as she crossed the room toward the dishwasher, she heard voices coming from upstairs. It was Tony and Delana having some sort of heated discussion on the upstairs landing. Her first reaction was to remind them to go to bed because they had school the next morning, but telling them what to do and when to do it was no longer her responsibility; it was their father's. But knowing how tired and worn-out he was, he was probably already downstairs in bed sound asleep and didn't even hear them.

Determined to stay out of whatever was going on, she headed back across the kitchen, stopping mid-step when she heard her name mentioned rather loudly.

Unable to resist listening to what they were saying about her, she softly padded her way through the darkened living room and crouched beside the stairway.

five

"If you would have put that dead mouse in her bed like I told you to," Delana was saying, nose to nose with her brother, "she would have been out of here by now, but no—you wouldn't listen to me. You had a better idea."

"She'd know in a minute it was me who put it there and go running to Dad. I think we had better just keep messing up the things she cleans, argue with her, be brats, call her names, that kind of stuff. You should have seen the look on her face when I called her a—" His voice fell to a whisper.

Delana let loose a belly laugh. "You actually called her that? What did she do?"

"Just acted like she was all upset and told me no one ever talked to her that way before."

"Do you think she told Dad?"

Tony snorted. "I dunno. But I thought for sure she'd quit after we smeared jelly all over the kitchen cabinets and did that other stuff. I kinda felt sorry about it, knowing how hard she worked to get it clean."

"I didn't feel sorry about it. I want things back like they were when Grandma was here. That old lady was so drunk all day she didn't have any idea what we were doing and she sure didn't care. She might as well have crawled into that bottle of hers for all the good she was around here. I don't know why I bothered going in and out of my window when I wanted to leave. I could have walked right over her and out the front door and she wouldn't have known the difference."

"So what do we do next? Doing all this other stuff sure

hasn't made her leave."

"Maybe we could take money out of Dad's billfold while he's asleep then tell him that we saw Tassie take it."

"You think he'd believe us? If we both told the same story and didn't slip up?"

"Probably. We could plant the money in her room. That'd be even more convincing," Delana added, lowering her voice a notch.

"Oh, I like that idea. What else?"

"I don't know. I'll have to think about it but we can't let up. We have to keep pushing her. No stranger is going to come in *my* home and tell *me* what to do. I want my freedom back. I can't stand having someone breathing down my neck."

"Yeah, me neither."

"Well, go on to bed, Tony, there's nothing else we can do tonight. But don't forget to mess up your room really bad before you leave for school in the morning. I'll make sure the bathroom is a total disaster before I leave. That'll tick her off. And let's hang out with our friends until about the time Dad gets home so she'll be worried about us. We'll show up just in time for supper."

"Good thinking."

Tassie stayed crouched until she heard both bedroom doors click shut, so upset by what she heard she could barely stand it. *They're actually working together to run me off? Maybe I should stay after all. What those kids need is a dose of good old-fashioned discipline administered in Christian love, and it appears I'm the one God has sent into this home to give it to them. At least for the next three months.*

When she reached her room, the first thing she took note of was her Bible lying open on the table. Placing both hands on it and bowing her head, she began to pray aloud. "Lord, You sent me to this home to be a witness for You. Please, I don't

want to just put in my time until the three months are up—I
truly want to win the Drummond family into Your kingdom.
Even when the children are giving me fits and I want to turn
tail and run, give me strength and make me remember that
this is where You want me to be. I don't want to simply tolerate
Tony and Delana and Babette; I want to love them as You
would have me love them, but I can't do it alone. Sometimes—
most of the time—those kids have been just plain unlovable. I
need Your help, Father God. Mr. Drummond needs You, too.
From the few things he has said, I get the feeling at one time
he may have been close to You. Speak to his heart and bring
him back into Your fold, please."

❧

Tassie awoke a full half hour before her alarm went off the
next morning and was in the kitchen, stirring the scrambled
eggs, when Mitch came into the room, still looking tired and
haggard.

"Good morning," he greeted her, none too enthusiastically.
"I've already made out your check. It's downstairs in my
room."

"Forget about the check." She took on a smile. "I've changed
my mind. If you'll have me, I'm staying."

His expression brightened. "Really? You're staying? That's
the best news I've had in a long time. You were so determined
to leave. Did something happen to make you change your
mind?"

"Umm, let's just say after our talk last night, I began to see
things differently."

"Differently?"

"Yes. I'm staying for you, Mis—Mitch. You're a good man.
I know your heart is in the right place when it comes to your
family. Even though your children have made it perfectly
clear they don't want me here, I've decided it really isn't *me*

they don't want, it's *anyone* who would come into their home, invade their privacy, and attempt to discipline them. But I'm willing to give it my best shot *if* you're willing to back me up—when discipline becomes necessary," she added quickly. Having his support was paramount. No way were his children going to listen to and obey her without it.

"You will back me up, won't you?" Having said all she had to say, Tassie pulled a mug from an upper cabinet and poured him a cup of the freshly perked coffee. The ball was in his court now.

He nodded his thanks then took a slow, careful sip. "Of course I'll back you up. I hate to admit it, but I know my kids are monsters. I've let them go way too far and for far too long, because I felt sorry for them having their mother walk out on them like she did, and then losing her in that accident."

"She walked out on you?"

"Yes, I should have told you up front. If I had, maybe you'd better understand my children's attitudes. Babette doesn't remember much about her leaving, but Delana and Tony do. June ran away with her biker boyfriend. Apparently they had been having an affair for months and I hadn't even realized it. And once she left, even though we always hoped she'd come back, we never saw her again. Less than a year later, they both died when a car hit them on a mountain road."

Tassie gasped. "How awful for all of you."

"And since I'm being honest about my wife, I'll admit I went into a depression when she left me. I know that's no excuse. I'm those children's father, but despite the way she treated us, I still loved her. Regardless of what I was going through, I should have been there for them. Instead, I backed away and threw myself into my work, letting my mother-in-law move in and take over. During the few years she was with us and I left them in her care, there were weeks at a time when I barely even saw my kids. If I got home at all, it was usually after they were in bed and I left before they got up in the morning. I'm not proud of what I did. I realize it was a mistake, but I can't go back and undo it. I remember someone saying you can't unring a bell, and I can't get back those years I lost with my children."

He looked so pitiful Tassie wanted to throw her arms about his neck and give him a hug. But she didn't. He was her employer and it wouldn't be right. Instead she simply said, "I'm sorry. I know it hasn't been easy, Mr. Drummond, and I'll do everything I can to help you get your children on the right track."

He reached across and patted her hand. "Mitch, Tassie. Call me Mitch. I feel like an old man when you call me Mr. Drummond. We are in this thing together."

She felt a flush rise to her cheeks. "Mitch."

"That's better." He took another sip then rose and placed the mug on the counter, taking time to bend and pat Goliath's head before speaking. "Don't let the rest of that coffee get away. I'll be back after another cup. But right now I want to go up and see my kids."

"Good idea." Tassie watched until he disappeared through the kitchen door. *Those children are lucky to have a man like Mitch for a father. A man who is willing to admit he's made mistakes and wants to rectify them. I just hope they realize it.*

Mitch. The word played on her tongue. She liked his name. It had a strong sound to it. "Come on, Goliath," she told the dog who lay at her feet half asleep. "We've fooled around long enough; it's time to get busy. The kids will be down for breakfast any minute now."

Goliath eyed his mistress then rose, and after arching his back and stretching first his front legs then his hind, ambled toward the door and whined to get out.

"Some help you are." She let the big dog out then closed the door and leaned against it. "Like it or not, I'm staying. For the next three months the Drummond home is going to be our home, too."

She filled the juice glasses, added the butter container and a plate of bread slices to the table, and was about to pull the milk carton from the fridge when Mitch, with one arm around Delana and the other around Tony, sauntered into the kitchen, a big smile on his face. "Breakfast ready?"

Tassie smiled back then gestured to the table. "Sure is. I've been keeping it hot for you."

"You'd better save some for Babette. She was sleeping so soundly I didn't have the heart to waken her. I was just telling the kids. . ." He paused long enough to pull out a chair for his daughter and seat himself. "That from now on I'm planning on being home by six each night so we can all have dinner together."

Tony huffed. "You've told us that before but you never made it."

Mitch covered the boy's hand with his. "I know, and I'm sorry. And I may not make it every night, even though I'd like to, but I am going to try. I love you kids and I want to be with you."

Delana responded with an indifferent shrug of her shoulders. "It's okay if you don't make it. We're used to you making promises you don't keep."

Their father's eyes narrowed. "Seems to me you kids also make quite a few promises you don't keep. At least I try to keep mine."

"Oh, yeah?" Delana challenged. "What about my birthday, when you promised you'd take all my friends out for pizza?"

"I told you I was sorry about that but it couldn't be helped."

"That's what you always say when you break your promises,"

Tony added, siding with his sister. "Your job always comes ahead of us."

"I don't have a choice, Tony," Mitch answered almost angrily. "That job is what puts food on this table, a roof over your heads, and clothing on your back. And money in your pockets to buy all the electronic and computer gadgets you seem to require, plus all the jewelry and doodads Delana needs to keep up with her friends. Not to mention the fancy cell phones I've purchased for each of you and the extra fees for your text messaging. Even your four-year-old sister has a cell phone. You kids must think I'm made of money. You have no idea what it takes to keep this family going." He turned toward his daughter. "Since you're going to be sixteen soon, maybe you should think about getting a summer job and start paying for some of those doodads yourself."

The young girl rolled her eyes in disgust. "You expect me to give up my summer and *work*?"

"Why not? I worked when I was in high school. I'll bet Tassie did, too. A lot of high school students work during summer vacation."

Delana crossed her arms over her chest. "Well, none of my friends work and I'm not going to, either. You're mean!"

She threw her spoon on the table then quickly rose, knocking her chair over with a loud thud, and stomped out of the room.

Mitch picked up the platter of eggs and handed it to Tony. "I know I've let you down in the past, son, and I'll probably let you down in the future, but from now on I'm going to do everything in my power to try to spend more time with you three kids. Meantime, Tassie is my representative in this home and I want you children to respect her and do what she says, because if you don't—you'll have me to answer to. Understand?"

Tony answered with a ridiculing snort.

Mitch reached across the table and grabbed hold of his son's wrist. "I mean it, Tony."

The boy gave his head a slight nod then yanked his arm away from his father's grasp and bolted out of the kitchen.

Mitch leaned back in his chair with a look of defeat. "Did I win that battle or did they? Maybe I was too harsh with them."

Tassie gazed at him for a moment before answering. "I'm not sure any of you *won* the battle but at least you're taking command. That's what's important. They may not be happy about it but as long as you let them know you love them, given time, they'll respect you for it."

"I hope you're right."

"So do I. You are going to make it for supper?"

"Yes, regardless of what's going on in Grand Island's crime world, I'll be here. It's time I started doling out some of my work to others instead of taking it all on myself."

❧

As promised, Mitch arrived home as he'd said with even enough time to take a quick shower before supper. After donning a clean T-shirt and pair of jeans, he hurried to Babette's room and tapped on the door. "Babette? It's Daddy. Can I come in?"

Within seconds the door swung open and Babette's smiling face appeared. "Hi, Daddy."

He lifted the girl in his arms and held her close. She smelled like lilacs. "You smell good. Did you just have a bath?"

She nodded. "I used some of Tassie's bubble bath."

Mitch glanced about the room. Everything was in its place, without a single shoe or article of clothing lying about. "You ready to go downstairs? I'll bet Tassie has a good supper waiting for us." When the child nodded he carried her downstairs. How long had it been since he had cuddled her in his arms like that?

"Tony! Delana! Supper time!" he called out over his shoulder as they reached the kitchen. "Tassie has everything on table." To his surprise both children came bolting down the stairs. Once they were all seated around the table, he motioned for Tassie to join them.

At first, she declined, but he kept insisting until she finally sat down. "I want you kids to realize Tassie is not our servant. For the next three months she is a full-fledged member of this household and we are each going to treat her with the respect she deserves." Then turning to her he smiled. "Tassie, the fried chicken smells wonderful. Would you please ask the blessing?"

Although she seemed surprised by his request, without missing a beat she prayed. How good it felt to hear someone pray who seemed to have a close relationship with God and could talk to Him in such a personal way. Other than a few desperate words sent heavenward now and then when troubles came his way, Mitch hadn't prayed, honestly prayed, in years.

"Can we eat now?" Using her fingers Delana snatched one of the two chicken breasts from the platter, barely beating her brother who hurriedly took the other.

Mitch rolled his eyes. "Did the thought ever occur to either of you that there are others at the table who might also prefer white meat?"

Delana peeled off the skin, took a big bite, and snickered. "First come, first serve," she mumbled, her mouth still full.

Tassie frowned. "Next time, instead of getting a whole fryer, maybe I should get just chicken breasts."

It was obvious to Mitch she was trying to avoid controversy over such a trivial thing. Maybe he should, too.

"Maybe that would be best, so long as you also purchase a leg or two." He nodded toward Delana. "Why don't you share that breast with your sister? Babette likes white meat, too."

Delana complied begrudgingly.

He picked up the serving fork, and speared a leg. "I'm a dark meat man myself. How about you, Tassie? Which piece do you prefer?"

He was relieved when she said she also liked the breast but liked a leg or the thigh almost as well. He feared, just to keep the peace, she was settling for a thigh when she would rather have had a portion of a breast.

Tassie smiled then reached for the bowl of mashed potatoes. "I made gravy, too."

"Mmm, homemade gravy. My mom used to make gravy," Mitch said. "I haven't had homemade gravy since she passed away."

"I hope you like it. I made it the way my mom taught me."

He bit into the chicken leg. "Mmm, this is good. I like that crunchy coating."

Delana wrinkled up her nose. "What's that? In that bowl?"

Tassie pushed the bowl toward her. "At our house, for lack of a better name, we always called them chicken crumbs."

The girl turned her head away and made a face. "Yuk! That sounds awful."

Mitch took hold of the bowl and spooned out several of the largest crumbs then popped one into his mouth. "These are great! How did you make them?"

"They're pretty simple. After I flour the chicken and place it in the hot oil in the skillet, I take the leftover flour and add salt, pepper, and just enough water to make it like a thick paste. Then I drop it by scant teaspoonfuls into the skillet, filling all the empty spaces and let them cook and brown right along with the chicken."

Mitch passed the bowl to Tony. "You gotta try these, son. They're amazing."

Tony hesitated then slowly slipped one into his mouth and began to chew.

"So, whatcha think?"

After a mischievous grin, Tony pulled the bowl closer and scooted four or five of the beautifully browned crumbs onto his plate. "They're pretty good."

Mitch gestured toward the bowl. "How about you, Delana? Want to give them a try?"

"Never! Those things are disgusting!"

"I want one."

Mitch smiled at Babette. "Sure, honey. Here's a nice big one for you. If you like it, you can have more." After placing the golden crumb on her plate, he handed the bowl to Tassie. "If you want any of these you'd better get them now. I love these things."

She took two of the smaller ones. "I'm glad. I wasn't sure you would."

"Hey, those chicken crumbs are almost as good as the chicken! Promise every time you make fried chicken you'll make crumbs."

Delana rolled her eyes. "Do you have any idea how many grams of fat and how many calories you're consuming by eating those—things?"

Mitch chuckled. "Surely you didn't think about fat and calories when you grabbed that chicken breast off the plate."

"I pulled the skin off. I'm only eating the white meat and I'm not eating any of that fattening gravy."

He paused, then smiling, ladled a generous serving of gravy onto his mound of mashed potatoes. "Good, that means more for the rest of us!"

"Go ahead. Eat that awful stuff and get fat. See if I care!"

"Come on, Delana, I was only teasing. Maybe, since you're really into this nutrition thing, you could help Tassie plan the meals."

"That's a wonderful idea," Tassie responded with enthusiasm.

"She could even help me with the shopping."

"No way! I have better things to do with my time than spend it with our servant!" Delana rose then wadded up her paper napkin, tossed it onto her plate, and hurried out of the room.

Embarrassed by his daughter's behavior, he turned toward Tassie with a shrug. "Sorry, I guess that didn't go so well."

"You tried and at least you all gathered together for dinner. That's a start."

Tony glanced around the kitchen. "Any dessert?"

Tassie grinned. "How about Twinkies?"

The boy wrinkled up his face. "I had those at school. Two packages."

Smiling, she pushed back her chair and walked toward the refrigerator. "Then how about a nice big wedge of butterscotch meringue pie?"

Tony's face lit up. "Are you kidding? That's my favorite kind!"

She pulled the door open and reached inside, pulling out a beautifully browned meringue pie. "Then you're in luck! That's the kind I baked. I was only kidding about the Twinkies."

Mitch frowned. "How did you know that was his favorite? I didn't tell you."

She cut a liberal wedge, placed it on a clean plate, then set it down in front of Tony. "Lucky guess. I figured every boy likes butterscotch meringue pie."

Mitch eyed the luscious-looking pie as she cut another wedge, hoping it was for him. "You're going to have all of us spoiled."

Using the spatula, she placed some pie on a plate and handed it to him. "That's my intent. I love to cook and it's fun to cook when people appreciate it."

Babette took a final bite of the small piece of chicken breast

Delana had given her then pushed her plate toward Tassie. "I like pie."

Mitch watched with delight as his two children devoured their pie. Maybe Tassie's good cooking would be the way for her to win the hearts of his children. "Their mother rarely cooked. She said it was a waste of time. When she was alive, most of our meals were either eaten at a restaurant or delivered to our home." He smiled at her. Having such good home-cooked meals was one of the fringe benefits he hadn't expected when he'd hired Tassie to care for his family. How lucky could they be?

"A lot of women don't like to cook, but my mom always loved it. I guess I inherited my love of cooking from her."

"I'll help clear the table," he told her when they had finished their pie and both Tony and Babette had gone to their rooms, "just as soon as I finish the rest of this delicious coffee." He waved his hand toward the pie pan. "I'll eat that last piece later—unless you want it."

"No, it's all yours."

He emptied his cup, all the while gazing at her, then gathered the dishes from the table, rinsed them, and arranged them in the dishwasher while she put things in the refrigerator and wiped off the counter. In no time at all, the kitchen was spotless.

"I don't know what to think about Delana," he told her as they made their way into the living room. "Nothing makes that girl happy. It's like she goes through life looking for something to complain about."

He waited until Tassie sat down in one of the chairs then seated himself on the sofa.

"You need to spend more one-on-one time with her, Mitch."

"I know but she never seems to have time for me."

"Maybe she thinks you don't have time for her. You yourself

said you're never home. What about Tony? Have you ever made time for that boy? Like daughters, sons need their fathers."

"Are you saying I'm the one responsible for my children's outlandish behavioral problems?"

She shrugged. "You're their father. Have you made any real effort to get to know them—or Babette? She had to have been a baby when your wife left. That little girl needs her daddy. Can you honestly say you've been there for her? Just making sure a reliable babysitter is with your children isn't enough. They need you."

He leaned back and spread his arms across the back of the sofa and deeply exhaled. "What is this? Stack it on Mitchell Drummond night? Is everyone against me?"

"I'm for you, Mitch, but I've been doing a lot of thinking since you told me about your wife. Maybe more of the responsibility for their bad behavior belongs to you than you're willing to admit."

"Me?" His anger rose to the boiling point. "You've got a lot of nerve blaming me. I've worked my fingers to the bone to provide for this family."

"I'm sure you have, but the one thing they need most you haven't provided. A father who is always there for them! I know one thing for sure, when and if I ever marry, it won't be to a detective. Not if his job always comes before me and any children we may have. I'd rather be married to a ditchdigger. At least he would have regular hours."

"Look, lady, you can't march in here, spend a few days in my home, and tell me how to run my life. You've never even been married! What makes you an authority?"

"I'm far from an authority, Mitch. I'm merely stating my observations as one who is genuinely concerned about you and your family. I hope you'll take it that way. I'm simply trying to remind you that time is slipping by. Delana is nearly sixteen. Before long, she'll be gone, either to college or out on her own, and Tony is but a few years behind her. Unless you establish a good relationship with them now, while they're under your roof, you may never have one with them. A good relationship means having respect for one another. Just ask yourself, do your children have respect for you, or are you only the person who pays the bills, comes home occasionally when you're not tied up on some case, and lets them get by with their inexcusable behavior?"

He started to speak but stopped when she held up her hand to silence him, deciding to let her have her say before defending himself.

"And do you respect them?" she went on. "Those children aren't just disobedient leftovers from a failed marriage. They're your flesh and blood. You say you love them, but do you really? Because, from my vantage point, if you loved them as you say you do, you'd be with them more, even if it meant cutting down on the hours you work. You yourself told me you could have asked one of the other men to cover that all-night stakeout for you but you didn't, because you wanted to be there."

Mitch fumed as he listened to her accusatory words, but she was right. He had said that very thing. "You just don't get it, Tassie," he told her, gritting his teeth and trying to keep control. "Someone else could have taken my place, but no one can do my job like I can!"

She rose and stood staring at him for a moment. "You are so right about that, Mitch. No one can do your job like you can—especially your job as a father. I rest my case."

He lifted his hands in the air in frustration. "Okay, you're right. Everything you've said is true. I've known it all along. I just don't like hearing it from someone else! Does that make you feel better?"

"Not at all. My intent was not to hurt you, Mitch; it was to help you." With a roll of her eyes, she moved away from him.

"Listen to me. I sound just like my kids. Or maybe they sound just like me. I haven't exactly been a shining example for them. Their behavior does have a lot to do with mine, doesn't it?"

Her expression softened. "You said it, I didn't. Think my words over carefully. I'm going to bed."

He watched as she quickly moved into the kitchen then listened until he heard the outside door close. As his anger lessened and he calmed down, he began to rationally mull over the things she had said. Everything she had accused him of and everything she had said about him and his family was true. He had given his children everything he could except for the one thing they needed most. Himself.

Deciding there was no better time to start than right now, he tamped down what little anger remained inside him, forced a smile, and headed upstairs to tell each of his children good night and remind them how much he loved them—and that he would always be there for them.

Babette was already dressed in her Barbie jammies and sitting cross-legged in the center of her bed, the clothing and shoes she had worn that day scattered over the floor amid dolls and toys. Rather than scold her or leave them on the floor for Tassie to clean up, he picked them up and neatly stacked them on a chair. "So you liked Tassie's butterscotch pie?"

She nodded. "Uh-huh, I liked the chicken, too, and those funny-looking things."

He frowned. "Oh! You mean the chicken crumbs. Yeah, those were pretty good."

"Would you read me a story?"

Mitch gazed at his daughter for a moment before answering, Tassie's words ringing in his ears. He couldn't remember the last time he had read a story to Babette and he felt ashamed. "Sure, sweetie. Why don't you pick out the book while I go tell your sister and brother good night, okay?"

Babette let out a childish giggle of delight then leaped off the bed and began running her little finger along the spines of the books Tassie had organized on the shelf in her nightstand. "Hurry, Daddy."

He assured her he would then moved on to Tony's room and was shocked when he found the boy propped up against his headboard, hovering over a big thick book.

Tony gave him a startled look as he entered. "Ah—hey, Dad. You—ah—know anything about history?"

Both pleased and surprised to see Tony actually studying, Mitch pulled a stool up next to the bed and sat down. "I used to love history, why? Do you have a question about something?"

"Yeah, kinda. Did George Washington really cut down a cherry tree and then confess he did it or did someone dream up that story to make him look good?"

"Do you doubt he did it?"

"Yeah, I saw this thing on YouTube—a video a guy had made showing some other dude cutting down the tree and then blaming it on Washington, and when George denied he had done it his father whipped him really bad. That guy said a lot of the stuff we read in history books isn't true."

Mitch couldn't help but smile. "YouTube, huh? I don't think I'd take the word of some stranger on YouTube for what George Washington did or didn't do. I'd rather believe the history books. George Washington was a great president. We, as citizens of this country, owe him a debt of gratitude." Mitch wanted to shout with joy when his son looked up at him with eyes of admiration; usually they were filled with contempt.

"Thanks, Dad. I knew you'd know the answer."

"No problem. Maybe we can talk about this some more

tomorrow night but right now you and I have something else to discuss. Tassie was reluctant to talk about it when I asked her how her day went, but she finally admitted you behaved in an extremely ungentlemanly manner toward her. Did you?"

"Yeah, sorta, I guess. But she's always messing around with my stuff. Nobody touches my stuff and gets by with it."

Mitch did an exaggerated glance about the room. "You mean the *stuff* that used to cover the furniture and floor in here? The *stuff* I no longer see because Tassie went to all the trouble to put it away for you? Something you should have done yourself? That the *stuff* you mean?"

Tony crinkled up his face. "Yeah, but that stuff was mine. She's got no business snooping around in here."

"She wasn't snooping. What she did took work, hard work, work you should have done yourself. Besides, you don't have anything in your room you wouldn't want found, do you?"

Tony growled, "No, of course not."

"Good, I'd hoped not, but I am interested in hearing whatever you said to her. It seems she was hurt and offended by it. I'd like to hear those comments from you."

The boy shrugged. "Aw, Dad, it wasn't such a big deal. She's making too much of it."

"*If* the things you said were as common as you imply, then I'm sure you'll have no trouble telling me what they were."

His head lowered, Tony pursed his lips tightly together.

"Tony, I have no intention of going out of this room until you tell me, and don't leave anything out. I want to hear every word."

"All I said was she was a nosy old witch and had no business being in our home, that you would never have hired her if you hadn't been desperate."

"That's all you said?"

"Yeah—well maybe a little bit more."

"How could you say something like that to someone who was trying to help you? No wonder she was hurt! She had every right to be. I—I don't know what to do with you, Tony. Because of you children's outrageous behavior, Tassie decided to quit after being here only two days!"

"Quit? She's leaving?"

The weird smile of satisfaction that broke across his son's face ripped at Mitch's heart. It was as if Tony was proud of his part in getting Tassie to quit.

"Wouldn't you quit? If someone treated you as badly as you've treated her?"

"I—I dunno. Maybe."

"Well, fortunately, for some unknown reason, she changed her mind and decided to stay. She's not leaving after all." *Unless she got so upset with me and the way I talked to her tonight that she changed her mind again.*

His intention when he had come into this room had been to tear down fences, but he had to stand up for Tassie. He couldn't let Tony's words of criticism go unheeded. He had been ignoring things too long. "Well, you'd better get to bed. Want me to put that book on your desk for you?"

"No. I want to finish this chapter first."

Hoping to show an interest in his son and his schoolwork, Mitch leaned over, intending to simply see what period of history his son was studying, but what he found folded into the page was a nude picture torn from a girly magazine.

"Tony!" he railed at his son, yanking the picture from the book and ripping it to shreds.

"It's not mine, Dad. It belongs to a friend. I was just keeping it for him."

"Surely you don't think I'm dumb enough to believe that old line." Deciding he'd had about all the confrontation he could take for one night and not sure if he should lecture the boy, take away his allowance, or punish him in some other way, he simply stared at Tony for a moment then walked toward the door before turning back to the boy. "I'm disgusted by this, Tony, and believe me, this incident is going to be dealt with as soon as I decide how to punish you. There is no place for porn in this house. If you have any more of it hidden away, I suggest you get rid of it immediately because from now on your room is subject to search at anytime. If it is here—I'll find it and you'll wish you'd never heard of that filthy stuff. What you see and read in those magazines is nothing but trash and not at all like real life. Understand?"

His eyes as wide as saucers, Tony nodded.

"Nodding isn't good enough. I want to hear you say it."

"Okay, yes, I understand."

"Good. Now get to bed."

Mitch closed the door behind him then leaned against it, his heart pounding wildly in his chest. He knew from experience most adolescent boys were filled with curiosity about the opposite sex. He just hadn't realized his son would be one of them, and so soon.

Hoping to do better than he had with Tony, he moved on to Delana's room, only to find her pulling things from her closet and her drawers and throwing them onto the floor in a fit of rage.

"Do you know what that woman has done? I can't find a thing!" she yelled at him when he entered. "I hate her, Daddy! If you don't fire her I'm going to run away! I can't stand her touching my things and spying on me! She's evil!"

Mitch hurried to her, throwing his arms around her and pulling her to him. "Now, Delana, aren't you overreacting a bit? All Tassie has done is try to help you."

Placing her hands on his chest, she angrily shoved him away. "Help me? She threw my things in the trash! Good shoes and good clothes I had barely worn. She even took them out to the Dumpster!"

Since he was reasonably sure Tassie had simply put his children's items in one of the big empty boxes in the garage and not the Dumpster cart, he smiled to himself. "Come on now, I doubt she would throw those things away without good cause. Did you tell you *why* she was throwing them away?"

Delana sat down on the edge of her bed, her lower lip rolled down in a pout. "She said it was because she found them on the floor after she had warned—"

"Had you left them on the floor?" he asked, knowing full well she had. His daughter never put anything away.

A huff and a haughty toss of her head was his answer.

"She did the same thing to your brother's and your sister's rooms. She only did it to help you, Delana. Those clothing items cost money. Money I work hard for. I want you to have nice things but—"

"Then you should tell her to keep her hands off my stuff. She's the one who threw them away. Not me!"

"But if you toss them haphazardly on the floor—"

The tip of Delana's finger pointed angrily toward the door. "Are you saying it's okay for *that woman* to throw *my* things away? Just because I'd rather leave them lying around on the floor than hang them up or put them in drawers? I happen to like a messy room!"

Mitch cleared his throat with agitation. There seemed to be no way to answer that would appease his daughter. "I'm saying, my dear daughter, if you have any respect for me and the hard-earned money I spend on you, you would take care of your things to make them last. Throwing clothing on the floor and then walking all over it has to be hard on those garments. Is it asking too much of you to expect you to be careful with them?"

Delana avoided his eyes by pinning her gaze to the floor.

"I'm tired. I want to go to bed."

"Did you finish your homework?"

"No, and I'm not going to. I'm sleepy."

Mitch shot a glance toward her cell phone when it rang. "If you're too tired to do your homework, you're too tired talk on the phone. I suggest you tell whoever is calling you'll see them tomorrow." He stepped into the doorway and listened until she begrudgingly relayed his message to the person on the other end then hung up. "For your information, Delana, Tassie quit over you kids' bad behavior. But she—"

"She quit? Good! I'm glad. I did everything I could to make her know she wasn't wanted here."

"She *quit*—but after she quit she changed her mind. She's staying!"

The girl's face took on an intense scowl. "She's staying? Oh, terrific."

"Yes, and I expect you to make sure she continues to stay. From now on things around here are going to be different. I'm going. . ."

The girl screwed up her face even more. "Yeah, sure they will. Don't you ever get tired of singing that old song?"

Mitch released a breath of frustration. "Look, Delana, Tassie is the best thing that has happened to this family in a long time. We're—"

"She's nosy, Dad. She's always into my stuff! Why are you yelling at me? I can't believe you are taking that woman's side when I'm your very own daughter."

"I'm not taking anyone's side, Delana."

"Oh no?"

"Look. Having to adjust to someone new living in our home was bound to put a strain on all of us, Tassie included. But we each need to put our hurt feelings and pettiness aside and try to live together in harmony."

Remembering his resolve to be a better father, he smiled at his daughter. "Now go to bed, honey, and get a good night's sleep. We're all tired. Things will look better in the morning. Just promise you'll try to work with Tassie. If you think *she's* bad, try to imagine what the next nanny might be like. Take it from me, a good live-in nanny is hard to find. Especially one I can afford." He blew her a kiss then gently backed out the door, closing it softly behind him before lingering in the hall.

He was worried about Delana. She had been such a good kid before her mother walked out on them. Since that day it was as if she was out to make as many people as possible as miserable as she could, and he had no idea what to do about it. His shoulders lifted and fell in a despondent shrug. After taking several deep cleansing breaths and pasting on a happy face, he headed for Babette's room to read the story he had promised her.

But when he entered her room the child was already fast asleep, her bear cuddled in one arm, a book in the other.

As with so many things in his life, once again he was too late.

six

Tassie was pulling a pan full of beautifully browned pancakes from the oven when Mitch entered the kitchen the next morning with a cheerful, "Hello." She placed them on the table.

"Good morning, Mitch. I've been keeping your breakfast warm for you."

"The kids up yet?"

"Not yet. Since it's Saturday, I thought I'd let them sleep until you came up. I hope you slept well."

"I'd like to say I did, but I didn't. I. . ." He paused and cast his gaze to the floor, avoiding her eyes. "Everything you said about me was true, Tassie, but I should never have responded like I did. The truth is hard to face. I hadn't cared to admit it until I heard it come from your lips. I—" Mitch lifted his face to hers, a faint smile of contrition tilting his lips. "I'm asking you to accept my apology and I'm begging you to stay."

"Even if your children are doing everything they can to get rid of me?"

His eyes widened in surprise. "You knew Delana was doing all she could to get you to leave?"

"Yes, both she *and* Tony. They had not only proved it by their actions since I've been here, I actually overheard them making plans on how to accomplish it right after I had given you my notice and you'd gone to bed. I'm sure they thought I was up in my room. That's the reason I decided to stay. I couldn't stand the idea of letting a thirteen- and a near sixteen-year-old run me off, especially since I had prayed about coming

72

here even before I told you I would take the job. Did you tell her I'm staying?"

Mitch took hold of both her hands and smiled at her. He loved her fragrance. "I sure did. I made that part perfectly clear and I also reminded both her and Tony that I expect them to treat you with respect. I—I just wish I could guarantee they would do it."

She lifted misty eyes to his. "I do, too. It would sure make things a lot less complicated."

He freed one hand and pulled a paper napkin from the metal holder on the counter then gently blotted it to her eyes. "You have every right to be upset but please promise you'll hang in there. Don't let them get you down. I can't bear the thought of losing you—as a nanny," he hastened to add. "With your sweet smile and your desire to make things work. . ." He tacked on with a chuckle, "Not to mention your great cooking, they're bound to come around eventually."

"I'll only be here three months. That's not a lot of time."

"I know, and I'm going to do my part, I promise you. I may not make it home for dinner every night but I'm going to give it a royal try, honest I am."

She smiled up at him. "No one can take your place, Mitch. Only you can be their father."

"I know, and I'm going to be here for them—and for you. I mean—I don't want you to have to shoulder the responsibility alone." *What is that fragrance? Honeysuckle? Roses?*

"I can't tell you how much it means to know I have your support."

"I'll be here to back you up, Tassie, you can count on it. The kids need to see us as a united front."

Feeling the need to break whatever spell her presence was casting over him, he sat down and watched as she busied herself with the hot syrup that was simmering on the range.

"Want me to call the kids to breakfast?"

"Yes, everything is ready."

To his surprise, even though all three children looked as if they had just crawled out of bed when they'd heard his voice, they came on the first call, but only Babette wore a smile.

Delana took one look at the plate containing the pancakes and sausage and crinkled up her face. "More fat and cholesterol? I'm not eating those things. Didn't anyone ever tell you fat and cholesterol is bad for you?"

Tassie pointed to a clear plastic container on the counter. "I eliminated half of the egg yolks when I made the pancakes and I drained the sausage on paper towels."

"But they're fried. Can't you fix anything that doesn't have to be cooked in a frying pan?"

Mitch frowned at his daughter. "I will not have you talking to Tassie like that, young lady. Apparently you've forgotten the little talk we had last night. Apologize right now or go to your room and stay there until you're ready to apologize."

"Yeah, and what if I refuse to apologize?" Delana shot back with even more determination in her voice.

"Fine. Don't do it. It's your choice. I don't care if you have to stay in there until the snow flies, and you're not going to spend the day talking to your friends. Give me your cell phone."

Reluctantly the girl pulled her cell phone from her pocket and handed it to him. "You're being mean to me. I just might call Child Protective Services and file a complaint!"

"Look, Delana, I've let you get by with just about anything you've wanted since your mother left us because I felt sorry for you, but no more! Either apologize to Tassie or—"

"Never!" Her face filled with anger, she spun around and raced through the living room and back up the stairs.

❧

They all jumped in reflex when Delana's door slammed with

a bang, but Tassie had to smile when Babette held out her plate and calmly said, "Pancakes, please." She placed one big lacy pancake on the girl's plate then added some of the hot syrup and grinned at her. "There you go, sweetie."

Tony picked up his plate. "I'll take some, too. I don't mind fat and cholesterol." Although Tassie had to smile, not wanting to embarrass the boy, this time she kept it to a minimum.

Mitch nodded toward the platter then sat down in his chair. "Nothing is better for breakfast than a big plateful of sausage and homemade pancakes."

Once breakfast was over and Tony had gone back to his room and Babette to the backyard to play with Goliath, Mitch poured both himself and Tassie another cup of coffee then scooted his chair closer to hers. "I have to work today, but I already told the guys down at the station that short of a national disaster, I'm not working tomorrow. You should have heard them hoot when I said it was because I was going to church."

"You actually told them that?"

"Hey, don't look at me like that. I may not be as close to the Lord as I once was, but I am a Christian. I gave my heart to God when I was about Tony's age, at our church's summer camp. I wish I could say I've always been a good person like you, but I haven't been."

"What makes you think I've always been a good person? I've done things to separate myself from Him, too." The words slipped out before she could stop them. Even though God had forgiven her for her sin, she hadn't—and couldn't—forgive herself.

"Come on. Don't put yourself down to make me feel better. I'll bet the worst sin you have ever committed was being late to church."

Tassie felt her heartbeat quicken. "No, I've done something much worse than that, but I'd rather not talk about it."

He took hold of her hand and cradled it in his. "Whatever it was, I know God has forgiven you."

"Yes, He has." *Now if only I could forgive myself.*

"I'm glad you're going to be taking my kids to church." He turned loose her hand then gave her a smile. "I just hope when I walk in the door with you, God doesn't say, 'Who are you?'"

"I'm sure God will remember you. Have you told the children yet? That you're all going to church with me tomorrow?"

"I was going to tell them at the breakfast table, until Delana threw her little temper tantrum. I'll do it later on when she comes out of her room. Or should I say if she comes out of her room? But right now I have to go up and have a little talk with Tony."

She gave him a quizzical look.

"Nothing you need be concerned about. It's a man-to-son thing."

Man-to-son thing? What does that mean? Did something happen I don't know about? But since he didn't seem to want to elaborate, she decided to put his strange remark aside.

"Delana can be pretty stubborn. She may not want to go with us."

He shrugged. "I guess we'll have to pray that she will."

She frowned. "*We'll* have to pray that she will?"

He met her frown with a teasing chuckle. "Where's your faith, woman? You do believe in answered prayer, don't you?"

"Of course I do."

Mitch rose then extended his hand and pulled her to her feet beside him. "Then I guess Delana will be going to church with the rest of us."

Tassie rolled her eyes. "You're incorrigible."

He gave her a teasing smile. "And you're beautiful, you smell nice, and you're fun to have around."

Not sure how to respond, she returned his smile then moved to the sink and began scraping out the frying pan. Finally, without turning to face him, she said in a soft low voice, "You're fun to be around, too."

His laughter rang throughout the kitchen. "Are you saying *I'm* not handsome and *I* don't smell good? I used my best aftershave this morning."

"That's not what I meant and you know it. I'm just not used to kind, handsome men giving me compliments."

He sidled up close behind her. "You deserve those compliments and more. Want some help with the dishes?"

Tassie's heart thundered against her chest as she stepped to one side and began to wipe the counter. When he backed away, she turned to look at him, not sure if she should laugh, say something witty, or just ignore what she didn't understand.

He lifted his hand surrender style. "Sorry, I didn't mean to crowd you. Ah, maybe I'd better be going." As if embarrassed, he grabbed up his briefcase from where he had placed it on one of the chairs and moved quickly toward the living room.

"I'll be home in time for dinner. I'd planned to have a talk with Tony this morning. . . ." He paused mid-sentence. "I'll do it later."

She eyed him suspiciously. Had something happened with Tony he hadn't told her about?

"If Delana tries to leave her room without apologizing, call me."

"I—I will." Tassie remained standing by the counter, her heart racing. *Father God, what is going on between the two of us? I've liked Mitch—a lot—since the day I met him and have had strange feelings every time I'm around him. Surely he's not having strange feelings about me.*

She fingered her hair. *He said I was beautiful. Only one other man told me I was beautiful, and that man hurt me terribly.*

I can't let Mitch hurt me, too. I'm sure his actions were nothing more than an attempt at being friendly.

ॐ

At exactly six o'clock that evening, just after her father entered the front door, Delana came out of her room and peered down over the railing at Mitch and Tassie. After placing his briefcase in the hall closet, Mitch strode up the stairs and stood before her. "Did you clean your room?"

She huffed. "Yes."

"Everything is hung up or put away?"

"Yes."

"Nothing on the floor that shouldn't be?"

"No. If you're through with your questions, I'd like to get something to eat. I'm hungry."

Mitch smiled, then stood back and gave his arm a wide swing toward the stairway. "Sure, but don't forget apologizing to Tassie is a part of this deal."

"Da–ad!" she strung out, her lower lip turning down. "I cleaned my room. Isn't that enough?"

"No, that's not enough. Either apologize or go back into your room."

Even from the bottom of the stairs Tassie could tell the girl's face had turned red with anger.

"Can't I get a sandwich and some pop first?" she whined. It was obvious the girl was used to having her way and this was a whole new experience for her.

Mitch shrugged. "Nope. Not even a bread crumb until you apologize."

Rolling her eyes, Delana stormed past her father, down the stairs, and stopped directly in front of Tassie. "I'm sorry," she spat out angrily.

He leaned over the handrail. "With a little more sincerity, please."

Delana, her eyes filled with fire, visibly sucked in a deep breath and let it out slowly. "I'm sorry, Tassie," she said, her voice dripping with an exaggerated sweetness that was almost sickening, her head turned so her father couldn't see the vengeful expression on her face and the way her eyes narrowed as she spoke.

Tassie gladly accepted the girl's apology. The last thing she wanted was to upset everyone so that none of them would go to church with her without Mitch having to drag them there.

He hurried down the stairs to join them. "That's better. By the way, sweetie, we're all going to church together in the morning. You included."

"Dad! I don't want—"

He raised his hand to stop her. "Come on, Delana, you might actually like it. You and Tony had better set your alarms before you go to bed tonight. Church starts at eleven and I want us to be there on time." He paused, then gestured in the direction of the kitchen. "I'm sure Tassie has supper ready. Let's all go eat. I'm starving."

seven

Tassie wakened even before her alarm went off the next morning, surprised she had slept so soundly. *No wonder I slept,* she told herself as she stepped into the shower and let the delicious, warm water sweep over her face. *I put in a pretty grueling day yesterday. Today has got to be better. I just hope the kids don't throw a fit about having to go to church.*

She hurriedly toweled off and dressed, making sure to add a bit of lipstick and mascara, then headed down the stairs and into the kitchen to fix her specialty—eggs in a basket. She had gotten the recipe from a romance novel she had read, titled *With a Mother's Heart,* where the heroine fixed eggs in a basket for the hero and his invalid daughter. She was certain the Drummond family would love them as much as she did.

The house was eerily quiet when she entered, so quiet she found herself tiptoeing around as she put the coffee on to perk and loaded the grill with long strips of bacon. Soon the aromas of both hot coffee and sizzling bacon filled the house. Hopefully, the enticing aroma would make it easier for the Drummond children to crawl out of bed and the day wouldn't start with another scene. She had no more than had the thought when, to her surprise, an alarm sounded in one of the upstairs bedrooms. *Good. I was dreading having to wake them up!*

But the ringing alarm was soon followed by the solid beat of some rock and roll tune, a beat so heavy and pronounced it vibrated through the walls. Tassie's hands instinctively went to her ears. Then from somewhere else upstairs a second rock and roll number began to play, even louder than the first. The sound of a door banging against the wall and a few unsavory words from both Delana and Tony as they confronted each other in the hallway, with each screaming at the other to turn down their respective radios, and the war between the Drummond children was on.

What a way to start our Sunday! Tassie bolted up the stairs and stepped in between them. "Enough! If you want to play that ridiculous music in your rooms, that's your privilege, but you simply cannot play it loud enough to intrude on the privacy of others."

Almost instantly, she felt a sharp sting on her cheek as Delana slapped her. Caught off guard, Tassie spun around and connected with Tony who immediately pushed her back toward his sister.

When Delana grabbed onto Tassie's arms she found herself staring at the girl, nose to nose.

"Don't you ever tell me what I can and cannot do! You're nothing but a maid in this house and don't you forget it!" Turning her loose, the girl whirled quickly around and disappeared into her room, banging the door behind her. A second later, her radio blared even louder—so loud it nearly drowned out Tony's music that was still booming in the background.

Tony, obviously surprised by what had happened to Tassie, stared at her for a moment then went back into his room, leaving her standing alone in the hallway. With her heart pounding in her chest and not sure what to do next, she simply cradled her throbbing cheek with her palm and walked back downstairs and into the kitchen. She turned the strips of bacon over and then, almost robotically, began cutting big circles out of bread slices, neatly stacking them beside the grill. In all her life, no one had ever slapped her. Should she go downstairs to the lower level, knock on Mitch's door, and tell him so he could deal with his daughter? He'd said he would back her up.

She pulled the egg carton from the refrigerator then stood staring at it as it lay on the counter. No, that would make her look weak, like a tattletale who couldn't handle the situation and had to run for help. *Running to Mitch will never do.*

It seemed she had only two choices. Turn tail and run, get out of the Drummond home, and never look back, or take charge herself, handling things the way she felt the Lord would have her do it. After lowering the setting on the grill, Tassie bowed her head in a quick prayer then lifted her head high and marched up the stairs directly to Delana's room. After a quick rap on the door, she pushed it open and faced the girl head-on, gently taking hold of her arm. "Delana, I know you have had a hard time of it since losing your mother and I am so sorry you had to go through that, but you need to understand something. I am *not* your servant. In some ways, I am now a part of this family. So for the next three months we will all be living under the same roof. You can accept the fact that I am here to stay until then and work with me, or you can continue to make things miserable for all of us."

Although surprised when the girl remained silent she continued on. "Every home has to have rules. This one is no exception."

When Delana rolled her eyes and tried to yank her arm away, Tassie slightly tightened her hold. "My rules are few but each one is important if we are all to dwell together in harmony. Number one. Don't ever hit or even think about hitting me again! And no swear words are to be uttered in this house at any time. No TV, music, Internet, or phone calls until your homework is done, and absolutely no music played loud enough to disturb others. Your room must have a semblance of order at all times. I don't expect it to look perfect, but no more clothes on the floor or draped on furniture, and your shoes at least should be tossed onto your closet floor. If you need help organizing your drawers or closets I'll be happy to assist. I'd love to be able to spend some time with you and get to know you better. I'd like us to be friends."

Delana responded with, "In your dreams."

Choosing to ignore her remark, Tassie continued. "The rest of my rules are quite simple but equally important. Curfew times will be met exactly, unless later times are preapproved before you leave for the evening. No boys in your room—ever. And don't even think about crawling out your window and shinnying down that tree again because if I find you even trying to get out that way, I'll have to have someone come and cut down the tree. And lastly, breakfast will be at seven each morning, at least until school is out for the summer, and dinner at six each night. I am counting on you to be there on time both times, even if your father isn't."

"But—"

Tassie lifted her free hand. "Hold it a minute. In addition to helping around the house with a few tasks now and then, you will be expected to babysit your little sister occasionally, when needed. And you may be asked to help in the kitchen and with other things from time to time, like helping me plan the menu, which I hope you will do cheerfully."

Delana glared at her for a moment then spit in her face. "Forget it, lady. No one tells me what to do!"

Stunned when the spittle hit her cheek, Tassie released her hold on the girl just long enough to allow Delana a chance to give her a hard shove, sending her flying through the doorway and into the hall. Before she had time to regain her balance, the door slammed and the click of the lock sounded. Heartbroken and discouraged, Tassie leaned against the wall and, using the tip of her shirttail, wiped at her cheek. *Well, that didn't go as I'd hoped. Now what do I do, Lord?*

"Tassie?" Although she could barely hear with Delana's music blaring from her room, she turned at the sound of Mitch's voice.

"I—I'm upstairs!"

"Did you know the bacon is burning?"

She rushed down the stairs and into the kitchen to find him pulling slightly burned bacon strips from the grill and placing them on the platter she had set on the counter earlier. "I'm so sorry. I—I got sidetracked upstairs."

He grinned. "No problem. I like my bacon well done."

She glanced at the deeply browned strips on the platter. "I'll do better next time."

His grin broadened as he moved toward the coffeepot and poured himself a cup. "Mmm, nothing like a good hot cup of coffee to start a guy's day. From the sound of that loud music I guess the kids are up."

"Yes, they are." She busied herself by adding the bread slices to the grill then breaking an egg into each of the holes she had cut, watching intently as the clear whites of the eggs began to cook.

Mitch walked up close behind her and peered over her shoulder. "Ah, now I see. I wondered why you had cut the centers out of that stack of bread slices. I've never seen eggs cooked that way before. Looks good! I'll bet the kids will love them. And I like the way you're browning the cut-out bread circles on the grill. Those will be great with jam."

Tassie nervously nibbled on her lower lip. *If they'll even come down to breakfast. And if they do, they'll probably complain to him how I got after them, especially Delana. By the time she tells the story her way, I'll probably end up looking like a monster and he'll fire me on the spot. He said he'd back me up, but blood is*

thicker than water, especially when it comes to one's own children.
"I—I hope they'll love them."

He nodded his head toward the stairs. "I think I'll go and hurry them up. We don't want to be late for church, and we sure don't want those—what do you call them?"

"Eggs in a basket."

"Oh, yeah, eggs in a basket. We don't want them getting cold."

She watched as he left the kitchen then waited with bated breath for the explosion she was certain would come as Delana and Tony gave their father their version of the fracas that had gone on earlier. But it didn't happen. Instead, the foursome entered and sat down at the table as casually as if the whole incident hadn't even occurred.

Still shaking from her bout with the girl, Tassie removed the cooked egg concoctions from the grill, placed them on the platter with the bacon, and carried them to the table.

Mitch looked up, brows raised. "You've only set the table for four. You are going to eat with us, aren't you? You're a part of this family now, at least until September." He grabbed hold of the empty chair beside him. "Please, Tassie, get yourself a plate and sit down."

"But I need to get the juice and the milk from the refrigerator."

He gestured toward Delana. "She can get it. You sit down."

Prepared for an angry reaction, yelling out how Tassie was nothing more than a servant and had no business joining the family at the table, she shot a glance toward the girl. But instead of responding in a negative, hateful way, Delana simply walked to the refrigerator, took out the juice and milk, and placed them on the table.

"You kids have to try these," Mitch told his children while using the spatula to place bread slices on each plate.

Delana wrinkled her nose and stared at her plate. "What are those things?"

"Eggs in a basket." Mitch smiled as he answered. "That's what Tassie called them. Now let's ask her to pray."

Grateful for being asked but deciding the fewer words the better at this point, Tassie bowed her head and said a simple prayer.

Mitch added a quick "Amen," then sliced off a big bite with his fork and popped it into his mouth. "Mmm, delicious. From now on, I want all my eggs fixed this way." He waved his empty fork toward his oldest daughter. "Taste it, Delana. Go on, take a bite."

He waited until she had placed a tiny bite in her mouth and began to chew. "Okay, what's the verdict? Thumbs-up or thumbs-down?"

The girl lifted a feeble thumb. "They're okay, I guess."

Tassie felt relief. She had expected a thumbs-down just for spite.

"I like them. They're good." Tony pushed his plate toward his father. "Can I have another one? Give me a couple of those bread things, too, and some more bacon."

Tassie couldn't believe it when not one person complained about the bacon being too done, but she had noticed Mitch had taken the worst ones and placed them on his own plate before giving the least burned ones to his children.

After filling his son's dish, he reached the platter toward the sleepy little girl sitting in the junior chair, her chin braced against her palm as her elbow leaned on the table. "What about you, my baby girl? Aren't you going to try Tassie's eggs in a basket? They're good."

Without lifting her face, she sighed. "I'm too sleepy. I wanna go back to bed."

"Sorry, you can't go back to bed. Remember? We're all going to church together this morning! Now eat your breakfast, pumpkin. You need to eat it while it is hot." Using his knife, he cut a small portion from her egg, forked it, then held it close to her mouth. "Come on, take a bite for Daddy." She slowly opened her mouth and unenthusiastically allowed him to slip it between her lips. "Now isn't that good?"

The child's eyes grew wider as she chewed. "Can I have one of those bread things like Tony has?"

"With jam on it?"

"Uh-huh." Without using her fork, the little girl picked up the slice of bread circling the egg and began nibbling on it, her eyes brightening and widening a bit more with each bite.

Tassie hurriedly pulled two bread circles from the platter and slathered them with the delicious peach jam then handed them to her. Babette took one small bite from each of them then placed them on her plate before taking up a piece of bacon. She didn't say thank you, Tassie noted, but at least she was pleasant. That was good.

Soon they had finished their breakfast and the platter lay empty in the middle of the table. As everyone rose, Mitch suggested they each carry their dishes to the sink before going to their rooms. Although his suggestion was met with narrowed eyes and a shrug on Delana's part, each person complied without a word.

Mitch turned and gave Tassie a wink as he left the kitchen. "Great breakfast! By the way, I heard some ruckus going on upstairs a while ago, especially the yelling between you and Delana. I almost rushed to your rescue but I liked the way you managed things. You're exactly what my children have needed. What I've needed. This household craves order and structure and, like I've already told you, I'm 100 percent behind you. Every rule you gave Delana is a rule I should have set and enforced long ago. If I had, perhaps we wouldn't be in this mess."

"Thank you, Mitch." His words of support and reassurance

were just what she needed to hear.

He let out a sigh. "I know she spat on you. Most people probably would have either choked her or quit right on the spot. All I can do is apologize for her. No one should have to endure such a distasteful experience. I can't believe how well you handled it."

"Handled it? She shoved me into the hall and locked her door before I could say a word. That isn't exactly what I'd call handling it."

"You handled it by staying. I'm sure my daughter thought you would pack up and leave after that but you didn't—you stayed and you even told her you wanted to be her friend. And when she saw you here in this kitchen, preparing breakfast, she must have realized you had no intention of leaving, that it was a waste of her time and energy to even try to run you off. Not that she won't continue to try your patience—she will—so will Tony and so will Babette—but please, Tassie, don't let them get to you. Those kids need the stability in their life that you're bringing to them."

"I want so much to help them, Mitch."

"And you are. Up until you came the only two women they were ever around was a mother who made no pretense at caring for them, who never once told her she loved them, and their grandmother, who was not much better to them than her daughter. Please don't give up on them. Think about where they're coming from. I'm finally beginning to realize how much losing their mother has affected them, and I didn't help any when I went into my own funk. Especially Delana. Being the oldest I'm sure she felt abandoned by her mother. Not once, but twice. When she left us and when she died. I know, because of their outlandish behavior toward you, they don't deserve it, but please—when you feel like you've had enough and can't stand being here one more minute, take a breath and remember what those children have gone through. You're a Christian, Tassie. Let your light shine before them. Let them see God's love through you."

His words humbled her. When she had accepted this job, especially when he had asked her to take his kids to church with her, she had felt God had called her to work in the Drummond home. Yet she'd been sworn at, slapped, and spit upon. Like Mitch had said, no one deserved to be treated like that, especially if she had done nothing to deserve it. Yet, inside, deep down in the recesses of her heart, a small voice seemed to say, *"Someone else was treated like that, Tassie, was sworn at, slapped, even beaten, and spat upon when He had done nothing to deserve it. Jesus, your Lord and Savior,"* and she wanted to cry. What she was going through was totally insignificant compared to what He had gone through. Her misery could never even compare to His.

Mitch walked toward her and wrapped a comforting arm about her shoulders. "Promise you won't give up on us. I—I don't know what we'd—what I'd do without you."

With the still small voice still ringing in her ears, Tassie lifted misty eyes and smiled at him. "I know God loves your children, Mitch, and He wants me to love them, too. No matter how bad things get, as long as you back me up and want me to stay, I'll be right here, doing my best to help your family in any and every way I can. I know from experience love can speak volumes when words alone fail us. I am going to love your children, pray for them, and be there for them, no matter what."

Mitch gazed at her for a moment before speaking. "No one could ask for more." Then lifting his face heavenward, he added, "Thank You, God, for sending Tassie to us. Having her here is like breath of heaven itself to this family."

As he removed his hand from her shoulder and headed

back downstairs to take his shower, she let out a long slow breath. *I, too, thank You, God. Now, please, give me the strength to face whatever this day may bring. Amen.*

She'd barely said the words when angry voices drifted down from upstairs. Tony and Delana were at it again. Yanking off her apron, she bolted up the stairs just in time to hear each one call the other by names that really upset her and made her want to wash their mouths out with soap.

Dodging flying hands and fists she wedged her way between them. "Stop it! Now! One more word and I'll take your computers out of your rooms!"

Delana's chin jutted out defiantly. "You wouldn't dare!"

Though her heart was racing, Tassie kept her face even, not about to show her whirling emotions to this girl who was just aching to challenge her.

"You do that and my father will fire you!" the girl shouted angrily.

"Your father has given me carte blanche to run this house and care for you children. If you don't believe me, you can ask him as soon as he gets out of the shower," she explained, trying to maintain an evenness to her voice.

Turning slowly, Tassie focused her attention on Tony. "Why can't you children follow my rules? I was hoping by making them it would help us avoid confrontations like this."

He gave her a blank stare. "I—I didn't know you had rules."

Suddenly she felt bad. She hadn't given him her rules, only Delana, and even then she had blurted them out with no real thought as to what the consequences would be if they were violated.

"You're right. I'll tell you what I'll do. I'll type them, print them, then post them on the bulletin board in the kitchen, and I'll make sure I leave at least one copy on your and your sister's beds. It would be a good idea to tape them inside your closet door or somewhere you can refer to them. If you need an extra copy just let me know." She pasted on a smile. "Now, go back into your rooms and get ready for church. I'm going to go help Babette."

As Tassie moved toward Babette's room she heard a sudden crash.

eight

Turning and rushing into the room, Tassie found Babette sprawled on the floor next to her desk amid a sea of scattered books, broken glass, and a crumpled lamp shade. The child was crying and her arm was bleeding. She hurried to Babette and gathered her in her arms.

"I fell!" the girl uttered between sobs as she pointed her finger in an upward manner. "I was trying to get my kitty."

Tassie's gaze went to the series of shelves mounted above the child's desk. The very first time she had entered Babette's room, she had noticed the big white shaggy stuffed kitten reclining lazily on the top shelf because it had looked so real. "You climbed up on your desk?"

With tears rolling down her cheeks, the girl simply nodded.

"Babette, you should have told me you wanted your kitty. I could have gotten it for you." She paused long enough to press a tissue from the box on the desk to Babette's cut. "That shelf was much too high for a little girl like you to reach. Promise me you won't try that again. I don't want you to get hurt." Satisfied that, other than the superficial cut on her arm, the child was all right, she carefully lifted her from the floor and sat down on the side of the bed, cradling the shaking little body in her arms.

Babette cowered against her, hiding her face in Tassie's shirt. "Don't hit me! I didn't mean to break the lamp!"

"Hit you? Why would I hit you? I know you didn't mean to break it. You were only after your kitty." Why would the child think she would hit her? Was that the way her grandmother

92

had punished her when she didn't behave? Tassie gently tugged Babette away from her shirt and smiled down at her. "I don't think your cut is very bad. Would you let me put some medicine on it and bandage it up? Then I'll kiss it and make it all well!"

Babette, still sobbing, nodded.

Tassie stood and lowered the child onto her bed. "You wait right there. I'm going into the bathroom to get the tube of medicine and some gauze and tape and I'll be right back." She hurried into the hall bathroom and much to her surprise found everything she needed, even a small pair of scissors, and then hurried back.

Although the little girl said nothing the entire time Tassie was cleaning and dressing her wound, she sat perfectly still, her gaze pinned on Tassie's every move. After Tassie finished she kissed the boo-boo, returned each item to where she had found it, then lifted Babette in her arms and carried her to the rocking chair sitting in the corner of the room. "Would you like me to rock you? That's what my mom always did when I had a boo-boo. And you know what? It always made me feel better."

When Babette tilted her head and eyed her suspiciously, Tassie smiled at her, hoping to convey an element of trust. "We have a little time before leaving for church, so maybe we could read a book. Which book would you like?"

Babette pointed to one of the books scattered across her floor and seemed to perk up. "That one, about the baby."

Being careful not to drop her precious cargo, Tassie leaned over and picked up the book. Once Babette was seated comfortably on her lap with her arm resting on a toss pillow, Tassie opened the book and began to read.

"We need to leave in half an hour, and I know how long it takes women to decide what to wear! Are you guys about ready?" Mitch called up to them.

"Babette and I are up here in her room!" she called out, pleased he was eager to get to church on time. "She had a slight accident but she's okay."

⁊ⱥ

Concerned, Mitch climbed the stairs two at a time and stopped short as he entered his daughter's room. He took one look at the broken lamp then hurried to the rocker and knelt beside it, gazing with concern at Babette's bandaged arm. "You cut yourself on the glass?"

"She's fine, Mitch. It's just a surface cut. I think the fall scared her more than it hurt her. From what she said, I guess she tried to climb up on the shelf to get her kitty, lost her balance, and fell. Don't worry. Her arm will be good as new in a few days."

He rose and began pacing about the room as pangs of guilt assaulted him. "It's my fault. I'm the one who put that silly stuffed cat on that top shelf. I got tired of tripping over it every time I came into her room. If I hadn't put it there, she wouldn't have gotten hurt."

"You can't blame yourself. Accidents and falls are a part of every child's life. That's why God made them so durable."

Babette held out her arm. "Tassie kissed my boo-boo and made it all better, Daddy. Look, she drew a smiley face on the tape."

Mitch breathed a sigh of relief then gave Tassie a smile of gratitude. "I see, pumpkin. That was really nice of Tassie."

"Babette got ready for church all by herself. Doesn't she look pretty? And she didn't get one drop of blood on her dress."

He smiled proudly. "She's beautiful."

"Tassie was reading me a story. Do you want to hear a story, Daddy? It's about a baby."

He shook his head. "I'd love to hear the story, sweetie, but I have to make sure your brother and sister are getting dressed for church. Maybe you and I can read a book together tonight. Would you like that?"

She nodded then once again snuggled up against Tassie. "Okay."

He smiled at Tassie as he backed toward the door. "Thanks for taking such good care of my family."

"You're welcome. It's always nice to know you're appreciated."

He paused in the doorway and stood listening as she lifted the book and began to read. What a beautiful sight. His regret was that as long as that rocking chair had been in the house, he couldn't remember ever seeing his wife hold and rock one of their children in it. June simply hadn't been a demonstrative person. She required her space and resented anyone or anything that infringed upon it, especially him. Looking back, he wondered how they had ever come together often enough to even have children.

Oh, how he thanked God for sending Tassie into his life— even if only for three months.

ہ

"Smile," Mitch told his oldest daughter as he and Tassie and the three children seated themselves in a pew at Linwood Community Church. "I don't want everyone thinking I dragged you here."

"That's exactly what you did. I sure didn't come because I wanted to," Delana snapped back with a snarl.

"I didn't want to come, either," Tony added. "Only sissies go to church."

Mitch gave Tony a gentle nudge. "Make the best of it, kids. From now on, you're going to be here every Sunday."

Delana started to make a comment but stopped when her dad tilted his head in a warning manner and narrowed his eyes.

Although the children didn't cause a commotion during the service, it was obvious they weren't listening to a word the pastor said.

"Maybe next Sunday they'll feel more comfortable," Mitch reminded Tassie as the family made their way through the line at the local buffet restaurant after church.

Tassie nodded in agreement. "I wish we could get them in Sunday school so they could meet some kids their own age."

"Yeah, that would be nice but just getting them to church is a real accomplishment."

Later that afternoon while Babette was napping, Tassie typed her rule list on the computer then printed out one copy each for Delana, Tony, and Babette, even though the little girl couldn't read it for herself, and one to post in the kitchen. She even printed one for Mitch so he would know what she expected of the children, and then she printed a few extra copies as well.

When Tony came home from school the next afternoon, she led him into the kitchen and gave him the snack she had earlier prepared then sat down at the table and quickly went over her copy of the rules with him. He didn't say much but she could tell by the way he fidgeted and narrowed his eyes he wasn't too happy about them.

"Gonna go play some ball with my friends," he told her after stuffing the rule list into his pocket.

"*After* you've straightened your room, Tony. You left it in quite a mess this morning."

He scowled. "That's not fair."

"All I'm asking is that you hang up your clothes and clean up the mess on your floor like you should have done this morning. If you knuckle down it will only take you a few minutes."

"Then I can go outside?"

"Yes, but please, no TV after supper until you have finished your homework." She grinned at him. "Smile. Only five more days and you'll be out of school for the summer."

Snarling something under his breath he snatched up his backpack and stomped up the stairs to his room, slamming the door with a loud bang. Ten minutes later she heard the front door close behind him.

Delana came into the kitchen more than a half hour later, definitely not wearing the clothes she had been dressed in this morning. Tassie looked first at Delana's bare navel, then at the pleated skirt that barely covered her behind, then at the low cut of the flimsy see-through blouse she was wearing. "What happened to the clothes you had on when you left this morning?"

After raising one arm high in the air and striking a pose much like the models on the cover of the latest issue of some teen fashion magazine, she gave Tassie a sardonic smile that conveyed more than words could ever say.

"I asked what happened to your clothes."

Delana flipped her shoulder in response. "I traded with one of my friends."

Tassie's jaw dropped. "You traded them? Permanently, or just until tomorrow?"

This time Delana shrugged both shoulders. "Haven't decided yet. Might keep them. Might not." She did a mock pirouette. "They look good on me, don't they?"

"Delana, the attention girls get from dressing like that is the kind of attention you really don't want. You're not quite sixteen. What kind of a message do you think you're sending by exposing yourself that way?"

She shrugged again. "Who cares as long as the boys look at me?"

"I hate to put it so bluntly, but wearing clothing like that is the same as asking for trouble. I'm not saying that to scare you, I'm concerned about you, Delana. I don't want to see you get hurt."

The girl let out a snort. "The best thing you can do for me is leave me alone. I don't have to take orders from you; you're a nobody. If you are so smart and claim to know everything, why aren't you out working at a real job instead of being a babysitter? Anyone can be a babysitter. It takes no talent whatsoever."

Tassie wanted to grab the girl, throw her over her knee, and give her a good spanking—not because she had made fun of Tassie but because she was genuinely concerned about her. Somehow she had to reach her. There were men out there just waiting for girls like Delana. She didn't want her to end up as someone's play toy or victim. Deciding to put an end to their conversation, she reached for Delana's copy of the rules and handed it to her. "By the way, here's a printed copy of the rules we discussed earlier. Read them over and I'll be happy to discuss any of it with you."

"This is what I think of your rules." The girl ripped the paper into shreds then tossed them in the air and watched with satisfaction as the pieces fluttered to the floor.

"There's another copy on your nightstand. Probably be a good idea to keep them; otherwise you won't have any idea why you're being punished when you disobey one of them."

Delana's face contorted with anger. "You were in my room again?"

"Yes. Why? Is there something in there you'd prefer I didn't see?"

"No, but it's my room! You have no business going in there! Ever!"

"Delana, I don't want to go into your room. Like you, I wanted my privacy as a teenager. And you'll get it—just as soon as you show me you are a team player and can be trusted. With trust comes freedom. All your father and I ask is that you show us you can be responsible and that you are trustworthy."

"All you ask? Forget it, lady. My dad may be taken with you, but to me and my brother you're nothing. A big fat zero."

"Delana, as much as I'd like to have value in your sight, what you think of me really doesn't concern me as much as what God thinks of me. As long as my heart and actions are right with God, it makes very little difference what anyone else thinks. I am here at your father's request, to care for you and make sure your home runs smoothly. You can cooperate or you can fight me on every move, but I *am* here to stay."

Tassie paused, leaving time for her words to sink in. "So if you are as smart as I think you are, I'm sure you'll decide to go with the flow and cooperate."

After a loud "Ha!" that seemed to come from the pit of her stomach, Delana whirled around and left the room.

nine

Her knees so weak from the confrontation with Delana that she could barely stand, Tassie lowered herself onto the sofa. So far, even though she had made a bit of headway with Babette, she had alienated herself from both Tony and Delana. She hoped she had done the right thing by being so firm with them. If not, she'd really blown it. She considered going to her room to have a good cry when Babette wandered into the living room and scooted up close to her on the sofa.

"My boo-boo feels all better," she told Tassie, giving her a little grin.

"Well, then, let's kiss it again. Kisses always make a boo-boo heal faster." Tassie bent and kissed the child's arm just above the bandage then gazed at her. "I was just about to fix Goliath's supper and take it out to him. Would you like to help me?" When Babette smiled and nodded, Tassie rose, took her hand, and led her into the kitchen. The little girl held Goliath's dish while Tassie carefully filled it with the big dog's food. Then, with both of them holding on to the dish, they walked outdoors onto the patio where Goliath lay stretched out on his side under a tree, sleeping peacefully. He leaped to his feet when he heard their voices.

"I'll hold the dish if you want to pet him before he eats. It's always best to pet him when he isn't eating. Sometimes dogs get upset and nip if people bother them while they're enjoying their meal."

She watched as Babette placed her small hand on his head. "Goliath likes it when you scratch his ears."

Babette grinned up at her. "I wish I had a dog."

"You do? Well, I have an idea. As long as Goliath and I are living here with you, why don't you pretend he is your dog, too? I'd be happy to share him with you and I know Goliath likes being your friend."

Babette grinned then hugged the big dog around his neck. "Okay."

"But right now, I think we'd better give Goliath his supper so I can go back inside and cook supper for you and your family. Your father is going to try to make it home in time to eat with us. Won't that be nice?"

Babette nodded her head enthusiastically. "Maybe he'll read me a story."

"Your daddy loves you. You do know that, don't you?"

"Uh-huh, but I don't have a mommy. She went away with a man."

Her words broke Tassie's heart. Babette couldn't have been more than two at the time, maybe not even that old. Mitch hadn't been very specific about the timing. Did she remember seeing her mother leave that last time? How sad if she did. Not sure if she should make a comment or ignore Babette's words, she simply asked, "Would you like to set the table?"

Babette shrugged. "I don't know how."

After helping the child wash her hands, Tassie pulled a stack of five placemats from the pantry shelf and laid them on the table. "It's easy. Just place one of these on the table in front of each chair. Add a plate, one knife, one spoon, one fork, and a napkin." She glanced around the kitchen then grabbed up a candle from the built-in hutch. "To make our dinner really special we'll light a candle. Doesn't that sound like fun?"

Babette clapped her hands with glee then set about her assigned task, all the while smiling. "What are we having for supper, Tassie?" she asked when the last spoon had been placed and she sat down at the table.

"I put a nice roast in the oven a few hours ago. Can't you smell it? I think it smells delicious."

The girl sniffed the air. "I do smell it. Are we going to have mashed potatoes? I love mashed potatoes."

"I was going to butter them and add a carton of sour cream and chives but if you'd rather have them mashed, then mashed they'll be. If you'll help me, we'll add a nice big pat of butter on top and a good sprinkle of black pepper just before we serve them. That makes them look real pretty."

Again, Babette clapped her hands. "This is fun. I never cooked before."

"Well, I can always use help in the kitchen. You're more than welcome to join me anytime. In fact, if you like, you can be our table captain."

Babette puckered up her face. "What's a table captain?"

"Oh, being a table captain is a very important job. No one is allowed to set the placemats, dishes, and silverware on the table except the table captain."

"I want to be the table captain."

Tassie wrinkled her forehead and took on a serious expression. "Are you sure? Like I said, it's a very important job. You'll have to do it every night. That's a lot of responsibility for a little girl."

"I can do it. Please let me, please, please, please."

"All right, if you insist. I'll expect you to be here in the kitchen with me while I'm putting the final touches on our meals. Is that okay with you?"

"Yes, oh yes." Babette leaped from her chair and began marching around the kitchen, singing, "I am a table captain; I am a table captain," over and over, making up the tune as she skipped and jumped along.

❧

As promised, Mitch arrived home in time for dinner and was ecstatic when Babette rushed into his arms as he opened the door. He had never seen her so happy. She kept muttering something about being a table captain, which he didn't understand at all, but as long as she was happy, he was happy.

The wonderful aroma of roast beef drifted in from the kitchen. To a man used to eating in restaurants or having nothing more than frozen TV dinners or an occasional frozen lasagna served on paper plate, the thought of another home-cooked meal was almost more than he could handle. "Is that roast beef I smell?" he called out.

"Yes," came a voice from the kitchen. "I hope you're hungry!"

"I'm famished!" he called back in reply as he lifted his daughter and hurried into the room.

"We're having mashed potatoes. Tassie said we could. I get to put the butter on top," Babette said proudly, using her little hands to turn his face in her direction. "I set the table. I'm the table captain!"

"That's wonderful, honey." Then turning to Tassie he asked, "Want me to tell Tony and Delana supper is ready?"

"Yes, good idea. Everything is on the table."

Still cradling Babette in his arms, with a smile of contentment he headed toward the stairs.

❧

To Tassie's surprise, neither Tony nor Delana mentioned anything about the rule list or the run-ins they'd had with her. Instead they both sat quietly through supper, even bowing their heads when she prayed. Both even nodded their agreement when Mitch complimented her on the great roast and how he loved the way she had cooked the vegetables along with it.

"I'm the table captain," Babette stated proudly around her mouth full of potatoes.

Her sister leaned back in her chair and rolled her eyes. "Table captain, huh? Is that the way Tassie is getting you to do her job for her? By giving you a fancy title?"

Mitch let out a deep sigh. "Delana, why can't you be civil? That remark was uncalled for. I think you should apologize to Tassie."

Delana jutted her chin out defiantly. "Apologize? No way. Forget it!"

His eyes narrowed. "Now, Delana. I mean it."

"And what will you do if I don't?" she shot back, meeting his intense gaze with one of her own.

Mitch looked quickly to Tassie, as if he needed guidance for an answer, but she held her peace. As far as she was concerned, it was about time he began to take a stand and now was as good a time as any.

"Or—or—I'll cut your allowance in half this week."

Again, the girl huffed. "Sure. As if you'd actually do it. That's what you told me last week but you gave it all to me anyway."

"I might have done that last week but things around here have changed. From now on—"

Her eyes flashing, Delana leaped to her feet. "They've changed all right. You don't care anything about us kids, your own flesh and blood." She paused long enough to fling her finger toward Tassie. "All you can think about is *that* woman. What is it, Dad? Are you so hungry for a woman to take to bed, you'll let her get by with anything?"

That comment was the last straw. Tassie jumped to her feet, grabbed Delana by both shoulders, and stood toe to toe with her. "You have no business talking about me that way, Delana, and I refuse to sit here and let you talk disrespectfully to your father. It's about time you learned the world doesn't revolve around you and your wants."

Mitch tugged at Tassie's hand then stepped between them, his full attention focused on his daughter. "Tassie is right, Delana. You and your siblings have become spoiled little tyrants and it's my fault. I've been so concerned about giving you kids the material things in life I've forgotten what you need most—a parent who loves you unconditionally and loves you enough to discipline you and train you in the way you should go. You may not like Tassie, but having her here has shown me what the four of us are missing in life is a good stable home, where each of us loves and respects the other and where each contributes to our everyday life. Even though your mother isn't here, we're still a family and we need to act like one."

"But you're never home," Tony inserted.

"You're right, son, but I'm changing that. I've already let it be known at the station that I'm cutting down on my hours. I want and need to be home with you children." He lovingly slipped an arm around his daughter as he nodded toward Tassie. "Like we are tonight, all sitting around the table, having dinner together."

"And arguing!" Delana yanked away from his grasp. "How exciting. Maybe tomorrow evening we can all wear boxing gloves and duke it out."

Mitch's jaw dropped. "Delana! What in the world is the matter with you?"

Delana headed for the stairs. "What's the matter with you, Dad? Why all this sudden interest in your family? You've never cared about us before. Is this all *her* idea?"

He started after her but Tassie grabbed onto his arm. "I'm the cause of this. Let me go."

"But. . ."

Before he could stop her, she turned and ran up the stairs, sticking her foot in Delana's door before she had a chance to close it.

"Look, Delana, I don't know if it's me you don't like or if it would be any woman who intruded on this household, but I want to assure you of one thing. If I didn't personally care about you and Tony and Babette, I would have been out of here long ago. I can only imagine how hard it was to see your mother walk out on you and then lose her in that accident, but life goes on. Your father suffered a loss, too, a loss as great, or even greater, than yours, but being your father he's had to go on and try to make the best of things."

Delana plunked herself onto her bed, kicked off her shoes, and crossed her arms. "So what are you saying? That you want to marry my dad and be our mother? 'Cause if that's what you have in mind, forget it. I can assure you it's not going to happen."

"No, that's not what I have in mind at all. You know I'm going back to college in the fall."

"Unless you can snag him!"

Tassie had to work hard at controlling her anger. "To be real honest with you, Delana, no sane woman would want to marry your father and come into this home with the kind of attitudes you children have."

"Yeah? And we're going to continue to have that *attitude*, as you call it. We don't need a woman coming in here, making ridiculous rules and telling us what to do. You'll be here for a while and then you'll leave us, too, just like my mother did, my grandmother did, and even Mrs. Cramer!"

Was that a tear Tassie saw in Delana's eye? "Oh, honey, is that what you think? That those women have all abandoned you? No wonder you feel like you do." She tried to slip her arm around the girl's shoulders but Delana shied away. "Is that why you're so upset about me being here with you? Because I'll only be here for three months? But don't you see? I'm not abandoning you like you feel the others did.

I'm going back to college."

"But you're leaving!"

"Yes, you're right, I am. But we all knew that up front. I've never deceived you."

"My dad should never have hired you! I don't want you here."

Tassie realized she wasn't getting anywhere. Their conversation was going in circles. "Look, Delana, you're right. We're only going to be together three months but I have no intention of leaving until my time is up. I want you to know I'm here for you. You can come to me at any time, for any reason. I want to be your friend."

"I have all the friends I need," the girl spat out.

"Just remember what I said. The time may come when you need help from someone you can trust. I'm that person." Tassie turned and, even though tumultuous emotions were raging inside her, walked calmly out the door, closing it securely behind her. *I've done all I can, God. I'm out of ideas. I just don't seem to be able to reach her. The rest is up to You.*

As she moved back downstairs she could hear voices coming from the living room.

❧

"Tassie!" Mitch called out. "Come here. There's someone I want you to meet."

She smoothed her hair as she hurried into the living room.

"Tassie, this is my coworker and my best friend, Chaplain Dale Lewis. The two of us started out as beat officers and then we were both promoted to detective. Dale left the force about four years ago to attend Bible college. Now he's the police chaplain."

Chaplain Lewis, a pleasant-looking man with an oversized sincere smile, held out his hand. "Nice to meet you, Miss. . ."

"Tassie Springer. Please call me Tassie, Chaplain Lewis."

"Only if you'll call me Dale."

She smiled her agreement. "So you're a chaplain with the police department?"

"Sure am and I love it."

Mitch chuckled. "But he still carries his gun. Show it to her, Dale."

Tassie reared back. "That's okay. I'm not really interested in guns."

Dale smiled as he reached into the shoulder holster under his jacket. "You might be in this one. It belonged to my great-grandfather who was a sheriff over in Missouri in the late 1880s."

Mitch gestured toward the gun. "Look at the pearl set into the handle, Tassie. It even has his great-grandfather's initials and the year he got the gun etched into it."

She moved closer for a better look. "It's beautiful. I didn't know they made guns like that."

Dale smiled proudly. "There aren't many like this around anymore. It's a real keepsake and one of the most dependable guns I've ever used."

"And he needs that gun. As a chaplain, Dale deals with a number of seedy characters," Mitch explained as Dale slipped the gun back into its holster.

Dale gave his jacket a pat. "Mitch is right. This gun goes with me everywhere I go. I'm never without it. I also respond to a number of domestic violence calls. Those are the worst kind. I pray I'll never have to use it, but it's wise to be prepared." As if wanting to change the subject, he turned to Tassie. "Mitch tells me you're a believer."

"Yes, I am."

He nodded toward the stairs. "Sounded like you and Delana were having a difference of opinion when I arrived."

"Tassie is trying so hard to reach my daughter," Mitch

explained. "That girl shuts everyone out. Even me. I have no idea what to do with her. It's like she's mad at the world and everyone in it."

"She's had a rough time of it, but I don't have to remind you of what she's gone through. You've gone through it, too."

"And I wouldn't have made it if it weren't for you and your wonderful counseling. The many times we prayed together helped, too."

"You are praying for Delana, aren't you? Prayer is a powerful tool."

Mitch bobbed his head. "Yes, both Tassie and I are praying for her, but sometimes it seems as if God isn't listening."

The chaplain chuckled. "Oh, He's listening all right, but never forget: God does things in His own way, in His own time—but that doesn't mean He doesn't use people to accomplish His will. That's why He made parents. Just hang in there, pray, and show her your love even when she seems not to want it. Prayer is powerful and so is love. Team those two together and you can't miss." He sent a smile Tassie's way. "Maybe the three of us can get together soon and talk about it."

She nodded. "I'd like that. I really want to help Mitch win his children to our Lord."

"Good. I wish I could stay longer but, if you'll both excuse me, I really need to be going." Then, turning to Mitch he added, "I knew you'd want that report about Jeff Clarkson's family. They're going through a rough time right now with their son in custody."

Mitch followed him to the door. "Thanks, Dale. I'll give them a call. By the way, plan on having dinner with us sometime soon. Tassie is a great cook."

"You name the night and I'll be here."

Mitch told him good-bye then turned to Tassie with a look

of concern. "So how did you make out with Delana?"

Her shoulders rose in a shrug. "I have no idea. At least she listened to most of what I had to say. I guess that's progress."

He moved close to her. "You're not leaving us, are you?"

She mustered up a smile. "No, I couldn't leave if I wanted to. I told Delana I was staying. Leaving would admit defeat."

Mitch reached for her hand, then cradling it in his, brought it to his lips. "Delana didn't mean what she said. She was only spouting off. I'm with you on this. You do know that, don't you?"

She nodded. "Yes, I know, and I'm counting on it."

⁂

"I'm still amazed at how sweet and loving Babette is," he told Tassie one evening as they sat on the sofa, watching the evening news on TV. How did you ever get her to do such a turnaround?"

"I guess by just giving her the attention every little girl craves. I wish the attention I try to give Delana would work that well."

He shamefully hung his head. "That attention should have come from me. How could I have been so blind? I put my baby girl's material needs above her emotional needs."

The pitiful look on his face broke Tassie's heart. She turned and laid her hand on his shoulder. "You were hurting, too, Mitch. When your wife left you, you had to have felt rejection. Then—even though the two of you were no longer together—you lost her in such a horrible way. Granted, those children lost their mother, but you lost your wife."

"But I was adult. I should have. . ."

She met his gaze. "Don't do that to yourself. What is past is past. You can't change any of it. All you can do is move forward."

"What would I have done if you hadn't come along?"

"Me? All I've done is alienate your older children and cause an even bigger rift between you and them."

"No! That's not what you've done at all. I don't want my kids to be juvenile delinquents and I'm afraid that's the way they are headed. What you've done is given me the courage to take charge and let them know who is in control around here. To stand up and become the father they deserve."

"It's not going to happen overnight," she said honestly.

"I know."

When he scooted closer and put his arm around her shoulders, she didn't resist. She loved being near him. In fact, the time they had begun to spend together each evening, cleaning the kitchen after dinner, had become her favorite time of day. She loved the way they could laugh and talk together about the things that happened to him on his shift as a detective.

"I can't do it alone. I need you by my side in this, Tassie."

"I am with you, Mitch, but what you really need is to rededicate yourself to God. I can help, but as the spiritual leader and head of this household, it's your responsibility to make sure your family attends church and is taught the Word of God."

"I know, but sometimes my job. . ."

She frowned at him. "Come on, be honest. Did you really have to work all those Sundays in the past or was it because you were so dedicated to getting the bad guys off the street you let your job take over your life? Mitch, what you do is admirable. The streets of Grand Island are safer because of you, but your children are a gift from God. If He didn't expect you to be there for them He would never have given them to you. You owe them your time."

He gazed at her for a moment as if thinking over her words.

"I don't mean to offend you by speaking so bluntly, but no one else can take your place."

"Okay, message received. If I'm to be the good daddy I want to be I'd better go up and read that story to Babette before she goes to sleep."

"Good idea. I think I'll go to my room, call Mom and Dad, read awhile after I take my shower, then get to bed early. See you in the morning. Did you remind Tony and Delana that since tomorrow is Sunday, they'll need to set their alarms?"

"I'll remind them after I read that story to Babette." He leaned toward her and gently planted a kiss on her forehead. "Good night, Tassie."

"Good night, Mitch."

❧

The next morning, much to her surprise, all four members of the Drummond family were dressed and ready for church when she called them to breakfast. Even the ride to church was pleasant. Mitch looked good sitting behind the steering wheel, smiling and joking with her and his family. And rather than make their usual disturbance during the service, both Delana and Tony sat quietly beside their father and listened, or at least gave the appearance of listening.

"I really admire the way you openly worship the Lord," Mitch told Tassie when they arrived home after the family had enjoyed lunch at an Italian restaurant. "You know, it feels good being back in church again. I've always felt guilty for not taking my kids and making sure they knew the Bible, but not guilty enough to do anything about it—until you came along."

She gave him a shy grin. "And bugged you about it?"

He smiled back. "Yeah, I guess you could call it that, but it worked. Maybe there's hope for me yet."

"Of course there is. God never gives up on anyone. We may

leave Him but He never leaves us. I'm sure He rejoices each time He sees you back in His house."

"The kids behaved pretty well today, didn't they?"

"Yes, I was quite proud of them."

"Me, too. Who knows? They may even be enjoying it."

❧

The next four weeks went by with reasonably few confrontations, which both Tassie and Mitch attributed to putting Dale's wise advice into action. Tassie hoped the calm meant Mitch's older children were finally beginning to accept her. At least they were tolerating her presence in their home.

"Can you believe Tony and Delana are no longer complaining about going to church?" Mitch asked her one Sunday afternoon as he helped Tassie finish loading the dishwasher.

She closed the dishwasher's door, started it, then turned to face him. "And they've almost stopped harassing me. Probably because they see so little of me since they're out with their friends every day, enjoying their summer vacation. Mitch, I'm trying so hard to reach Delana, but she still shuts me out."

Their conversation was brought to a halt by the doorbell. "That's probably Dale." Mitch reached for her hand; then the two of them hurried to the door. "Good, you made it," he told his friend as he pushed open the storm door to allow him entrance.

"Hey, I'd never turn down an invitation to visit with friends." Dale paused and grinned at Tassie. "Especially since Tassie told me she'd save me a piece of her famous pineapple Bundt cake."

She smiled at him as she gestured toward the sofa. "You two go ahead and sit down while I get the coffee and cake."

She liked Dale. He was a good man, but more importantly he loved the Lord. Although she and Mitch hadn't invited him over specifically for a counseling session, they did plan to take advantage of his being there to ask a few questions and beg for some much needed advice.

By the time she'd filled the tray and headed back into the living room, the two men were deeply engaged in conversation.

"Mitch tells me little Babette has adjusted well to having you in her home." Dale stopped long enough to nod a thank-you when she placed his coffee and cake plate on the end table beside him. "But the older two are still not accepting you as part of this household."

"Unfortunately, that's true, Dale. I tried everything I can think of to reach them. I think Tony is slowly, but surely, coming around, but Delana is. . ."

"She's jealous of you, you know."

Tassie gasped. "Jealous? Of me? Why? She looks at me as nothing more than a servant. She even insinuated I had only taken this babysitting job—as she calls it—because I couldn't get a real job!"

Chaplain Lewis looked from Tassie to Mitch and back again. "Not the envious kind of jealousy. She is jealous of you as a woman—the woman she fears might take her father away from her."

Tassie felt a flush rise to her cheeks. "I—I don't know what you mean."

Mitch gave Dale a puzzled look.

"Oh, come on, you two. Don't try to tell me you aren't attracted to one another. You maybe have tried to hide it, but it's been pretty obvious. I've known it for weeks."

Tassie's hand went to her throat. *He noticed?*

"I'm sure, with all of you living under one roof, the children noticed it, too."

Mitch set his cup on the table with a thud. "Whoa, Dale. Tassie and I have never done anything improper. I've barely even held her hand."

"Knowing you both like I do, I'm sure that's true, but you have to look at it from your daughters' and your son's perspectives. First their mother abandoned them; then she died. That was like losing her twice. Next Grandma moved in and, although she was here physically, to be frank, we both know she was in a drunken stupor most of the time; then she abruptly moved out. Again, double abandonment. That would have been bad enough, but you abandoned them, too, Mitch. You literally turned your back on your kids and let your work take over as a way of dealing with your grief."

"I didn't mean to abandon them," Mitch said quickly in his defense. "I guess I just couldn't face reality."

Dale reached across and gave his hand a reassuring pat. "I know, old friend. Most men would have reacted the same way. Not only was your heart broken, your ego suffered a tremendous blow. But I'm proud of you. You've come out of it, you're doing all you can to be the father you should be, and you're taking your kids to church."

"I couldn't have done it if it weren't for you, Dale, and for Tassie's encouraging me to get the kids to church."

Dale gestured toward Tassie. "One of the smartest things you've done is bring Tassie into this home to help you. Having her here has to be a God thing. To be able to find a fine Christian woman willing to come into this home under those circumstances was nothing short of a miracle."

Tassie, not sure how she should respond, said a simple, "Thank you."

Mitch leaned back against the sofa and stared off into space for a moment before speaking. "You're right, you know."

She froze.

Dale gave him a shy grin. "About your and Tassie's attraction toward one another?"

Mitch swallowed hard. "Yes. I can't speak for Tassie, but I've been attracted to her since the first day she came to us. I know I shouldn't. . ."

Dale shrugged. "Shouldn't what? Be attracted to a pretty young woman like her? Why not? There's nothing wrong with two people who are not committed to someone else to develop a fondness for each other. I like the idea. It looks to me like the two of you belong together. That's part of the problem. Your children feel the same way. They probably noticed the attraction long before you two were willing to admit it. That's what scares them. They're afraid—if you and Tassie do get together—she'll abandon them like every other person they have ever loved and trusted has done."

Mitch gazed at him with a look of bewilderment. "So what should we do?"

"First and foremost—continue to pray. Fall on your face before God and ask Him to guide your every action, your every word. Next, be honest with them. Believe me, they already know what is going on in your hearts. Don't keep them in the dark. They may not like the idea of the two of you getting together, but they'll be more receptive to it if they feel like they are a part of it, rather than thinking you're trying to hide it from them."

Mitch rubbed at his forehead. "Are you saying we should tell—"

"Not *we*, Mitch. You. You're their father. At this point, Tassie should not be included. They need to hear it from you and you alone. Once you've told them, you need to sit back and listen to them, hear their viewpoint, let them know their opinions are valuable to you."

"So if they say they don't want Tassie and me together, we end our relationship?"

"No, not at all. That decision is up to you, but at least your children will feel like you were listening to what they had to say, that they had a part in whatever decision you make. But remember this. . ." He paused and looked at Tassie before turning back to Mitch. "It's what God wants that counts. Seek His will in this. If He wants the two of you together, He'll allow a love to develop between the two of you, a love that refuses to be denied."

"Even if my children—"

"Look, Babette has already become Tassie's shadow. It's obvious that little girl already loves her. You said Tony seems to be coming around. Do you doubt God can change Delana's heart, too?"

Frowning, Tassie said, "I don't want to be the cause of—"

Again Dale interrupted. "Tassie, this family was dysfunctional long before you came, so don't try to take on any of the blame. You told me you prayed about taking this job before you accepted it, and I know both you and Mitch are in continual prayer for his children. Plus, I know you are both children of faith. You have to do all you can to show them how much you love them, but more importantly, you have to turn it all over to God and trust Him. He is able to move mountains."

Mitch reached for his cup then motioned toward Dale's uneaten cake. "Thanks, Dale. We'll try to take your advice. But right now, you'd better let Tassie pour you a fresh hot cup of coffee so you can enjoy that cake."

Later that evening as the two sat on the sofa, discussing their conversation with Dale, Mitch gave Tassie a shy grin as he reached for her hand. "I'm more than attracted to you, Tassie. It may be premature for me to mention it, but I think I'm falling in love with you."

Awestruck by his words, she simply stared at him.

"I know I'm a bit older than you and come with a ready-made family, but do you think you could ever love me?"

"L–love you?" she managed to utter as her heart fluttered within her chest. "I—I think I already do."

He scooted closer and slipped his arm around her shoulders. "You have no idea how happy that makes me. Even though I didn't want to admit it, I've been attracted to you since the first day you came into our home."

She felt as if she should pinch herself. Was this really happening? "But—what about the children?"

He lifted his shoulders in a shrug. "Like Dale said, we have to turn everything over to God. If He wants us together, it will all work out."

They discussed their newly admitted situation for some time and the effects it would have on all of them. Then Mitch gave his fingers a snap and reached for his billfold. "I nearly forgot. I need to give you some money. Tony said you were driving him and a couple of his friends up to Wayman's Lake tomorrow so they could go swimming. Maybe you could take them to lunch at some hamburger joint when they get through. Knowing how boys can eat, I'm sure they'll be famished. You don't mind, do you?"

She took the bills and slipped them into her purse. "Mind? Not at all; it'll be fun, and I'm sure Tony will appreciate it."

"I heard Delana say she is going to spend the day at her friend's house, so I guess she won't be going."

"Too bad. Tomorrow promises to be a beautiful day. I guess it will be just Babette and me."

"Are you and Babette going to swim?"

Tassie let out a snort. "And embarrass Tony? I don't think that's such a good idea. Babette and I will be there to watch them but we'll do our best to stay out of sight."

"Just the same, I'm glad you'll be there. Did you ever swim at Wayman's Lake?"

"Yeah, I used to swim there all the time when I was kid.

I was even a lifeguard there the summer before I went off to college."

"Lifeguard, huh? You never told me."

Tassie grinned. "There are a lot of things you don't know about me, and I'm sure there are quite a few things I don't know about you."

He gave her a coy grin. "I'd like to know every little detail about you."

"Dad!" Delana's voice shrieked from somewhere upstairs. "I can't find my cell phone. Did you hide it from me?"

Tassie pointed to the pink cell phone lying on the coffee table then picked it up and held it out toward Mitch. "You want to take it to her or do you want me to?"

"I'll take it. Maybe if I start spending more time with her she won't be so jealous of you."

"You really think she's jealous of me, like Dale said?"

"What he said certainly made sense. I know I need to let the kids know what is going on between us, but maybe I should hold off for a few days. . .let things calm down a bit first."

She nodded in agreement.

"Dad! Did you hear me?" the voice from upstairs rang out again. "Did you hide my cell phone?"

Mitch gave Tassie's hand a hurried squeeze. "We'll talk later, okay?"

She nodded. "Yeah, sure."

⁂

"It's pretty crowded out here today. You sure it's safe for you guys to swim?" Tassie asked Tony as his friends began piling out of the minivan the next morning when they reached the lake.

He gave her a fierce glare. "Safe? You've got to be kidding. What do you think we are? Babies? You don't have to stick around. Why don't you leave and come back for us later?"

"No, we're staying. Your father will expect me to keep an eye on you."

"That's the lifeguard's job," he shot back. "Not yours."

Tassie took hold of Babette's hand and the two backed away, ignoring his disgruntled remark. "By the way, in case you and your friends got thirsty, I placed the ice chest in the back and filled it with soft drinks. There's also a bag of chips."

"We won't need them. Eric brought a bunch of stuff in his backpack."

"They'll be there if you change your mind, but please, Tony, keep an eye on each other and be careful." Determined to stay out of his way, she took Babette for a leisurely stroll along the water's edge, stopping often to admire the wildflowers and the natural greenery. Eventually, when Babette tired of walking, Tassie pulled out the old blanket she had brought along, spread it under a tree, and the two stretched out.

"This is fun," the child told her, smiling. "Can we come again sometime?"

"Sure, sweetie. Maybe next time you and I will go swimming. Would you like that?"

Babette lay down, flipped onto her side, curled up close, and yawned. "Yes, I'd like that."

"So would I." She began to gently stroke the little girl's back and soon Babette was fast asleep. Tassie gazed at the child, now so peaceful and lovable, and not at all like the raving little tyrant who had ordered her out of her room that first day. She turned her attention to where Tony and his friends were jostling out at the end of the long dock, and trying to shove one another into the water.

Tassie laughed at their antics until Tim, a boy much larger in stature than the others, the apparent bully of the group, began struggling with Tony. The boy was being far too aggressive and Tony appeared to be wearing out. She wished he would just jump in and get it over with before someone got hurt. The big kid's playfulness was getting out of hand. Finally, after one mighty shove, both Tony and the boy fell off. The other boys continued to jostle with one another, but as she watched, she realized Tony wasn't anywhere in sight. Was he simply treading water on the opposite side, or was he in trouble?

Unable to stand it any longer, Tassie leaped to her feet and, while both calling out Tony's name and praying, ran the length of the dock. When he didn't answer, instinctively, Tassie leaped into the water and began frantically searching the area in hopes of finding him. But Tony wasn't there! And he wasn't with the other boys. After sucking in a big breath, she dove under the murky water, flailing her arms and hands in search of him. When at last she surfaced, she screamed out for help, but both the crowd and Tony's friends were yelling and being so rowdy they didn't hear her, and the lifeguard was down the beach, breaking up a fight going on between another group of boys.

She dove again, screaming for help each time before she sucked in another breath and dove down, but no one was paying any attention to her. She couldn't waste precious time. It was up to her to find him.

For a brief moment, she thought she felt something brush against her arm.

But her air was gone.

She had no choice but to resurface or risk drowning, herself.

ten

With both her energy and her air nearly spent, Tassie gasped for air as her face hit the surface. "Help! Someone help!" *God, please! Please, oh please, help me find Tony!*

Sucking in the biggest breath her lungs would allow, she dove again. She was about to resurface when her fingers came in contact with his face. Grabbing hold of his arm, she used her free hand to fight her way to the surface and screamed out again for help. This time her shrill cry caught the attention of three of Tony's friends who immediately jumped into the water and helped her pull his limp body to the shore.

Tassie moved into position over Tony and, using the skills she had learned in lifeguard training, began CPR. In between breaths she glanced in Babette's direction and mercifully found the child still sound asleep, totally unaware of her brother's plight. "You, Jimmy," she told the third boy, "go to the car, get my cell phone, call 911, and tell them we need an ambulance and a rescue team!"

In desperation, she kept working on Tony, all the while praying. When a noise, an almost guttural sound, came from Tony's throat, his head gave a slight jerk to the left, and he gasped for air, she shouted a loud, "Hallelujah, praise the Lord!"

As Tony's breathing evened out, she lifted his slim frame and cradled him in her arms. "Relax, Tony. You're okay now. You have a cut on your cheek that will probably need stitches but, thank God, it looks like you're going to be all right."

The boy stared up at her with glassy eyes then glanced around. "What happened?"

"You must have hit your head when you fell off the dock."

"Tassie pulled you out," one of Tony's friends explained with widened eyes.

"Tassie!" Babette screamed out as she wakened from her nap and began to cry.

Another of Tony's friends brought Babette to Tassie, who then explained to her as best she could what had happened to her brother. "But don't worry. He's going to be fine."

Suddenly, off in the distance, she heard the wail of a siren. By the time the ambulance and rescue crew roared into the parking area, Tony's breathing had returned to near normal and he was sitting up on his own.

One of the EMTs quickly knelt beside him, and after asking a few questions and checking him out, gave him a thumbs-up. "Everything seems okay, but since that gash on your cheek will require a few stitches, we'll take you to St. Francis Med Center and let them have a look at you."

"Is Tony going to ride in the am-a-lance?" Babette asked, wide-eyed.

Tassie gave her a reassuring smile. "Yes, the doctor needs to take care of that cut."

"Can I ride in the am-a-lance with him? I never went in an am-a-lance."

"No, honey, you have to ride home with me. You wouldn't want me getting lonely, would you? Besides, we have to take Tony's friends to their homes and tell their parents what happened."

Babette smiled up at her. "Okay. I'll ride with you."

Knowing Mitch had to be told about Tony's accident, as soon as the ambulance pulled out of the parking lot, Tassie dialed his cell phone only to get his voice mail. She certainly didn't want to leave bad news like that in a message. Mitch would freak out, so she simply told him to call her as soon as he got her message. After that she called the station and was told he was out on a case and currently unreachable.

She had barely broken the connection when her phone rang and Mitch's number came up on the ID. "Oh, Mitch, Tony had an accident at Wayman's Lake, but he's okay. The am—"

"Accident? What kind of accident? What happened?"

"He and his friends were at the end of that long dock, trying to shove one another into the water. That big kid, you know the one I mean, the Grisham boy—he got pretty rough with Tony and when he shoved him in, Tony either hit his head on the dock or one of the pilings and it knocked him out."

"But he's okay? Someone got to him in time to pull him out?"

"Yes. The EMTs checked him over and they said he looked fine but they took him to St. Francis to make sure and to have his cheek looked at. It'll require stitches. I wanted to go with him but Babette is with me and someone has to take his friends home. Oh, Mitch, I've never been so scared."

"I need to get to him. You and Babette go ahead and take the boys home. I'll stay with Tony until they release him. And, sweetheart, thanks for being there for him. I'll see you as soon as we get home." He paused. "Tassie?"

He called me sweetheart! "Yes?"

"I—I love you."

Her heart reeling at his unexpected words, she found herself almost unable to speak. "I—I think I love you, too."

"Thanks for being there for my boy, and for being with Babette."

"You're welcome. I—I'm glad I was there."

Once her mind began to settle down again, a wave of thankfulness washed over her as she gave in to reality. Tony could have died if she hadn't gotten to him in time. But praise the Lord, God had answered her prayers. What an awesome God she served. And if that wasn't enough, the man of her dreams had declared his love for her.

❧

Delana sauntered into the living room when Tassie and Babette entered the house. "It's about time you got home. I was beginning to wonder if we were going to have to go without supper."

"Tony had an accident while he was swimming. He nearly drowned," she explained. "The EMT said he thought he was going to be okay, but they took him to the hospital. He sustained a nasty cut on his cheek that probably required stitches, and they wanted to check him out. Your father went to the hospital to be with him."

The girl rolled her eyes. "That sounds like something my klutzy brother would do. He's always doing something stupid."

It upset Tassie to see how unconcerned the girl was about her brother, especially when she simply shrugged and went to her room without asking any more questions. How could she be so heartless?

It was nearly eight before Mitch arrived home, and Tony was with him, the side of his face covered by a big white bandage. Tassie nearly went into shock when Tony hurried to her and gave her a feeble hug. "Dad said I should thank you for jumping in after me."

Mitch rushed to the pair and circled them with his long arms. "The EMT told us it was you who saved my son's life, Tassie. Why didn't you tell me you were the one who found him and pulled him out?"

As he pressed his head against hers she felt tears fall onto her cheek.

"All I did was jump in the water and search for him. It was God who led me to him. You wouldn't believe how hard I prayed."

Tony gave her a shy smile. "I'm glad you found me."

She placed a gentle hand on his shoulder. "I'm sorry about your cheek. Does it hurt very much?"

"It's okay. Good thing you stayed at the lake when I told you to go home."

Mitch pulled back and stared at Tony. "You told her to leave? Why?"

"Because all the guys made fun of me, Dad. They called her my babysitter."

"I'm glad you realize your *babysitter* is the one who saved your life while your so-called friends were all too busy having fun to realize you were in trouble. Tassie was pretty brave to leap into that water and search for you like she did. Especially after the way you've treated her. Maybe now you two can become friends."

Mitch gave Tassie a wink, and wrapping an arm about his son, tugged Tony toward the stairway. "But right now off to bed with you, kiddo. You've had a busy day. I'm sure you're exhausted."

"I could fix you both a sandwich," Tassie volunteered, gesturing toward the kitchen.

"Thanks, but we went through the drive-through on the way home and picked up a hamburger."

She fought back tears as she watched them walk away. Realizing Tony was missing and then diving into that water, not knowing if she would find him or not, had taken its toll on her, too. Now that they were all safely back home and things had nearly returned to normal, every bone and muscle in her body ached. All she wanted was to finish loading the dishwasher then get a cool drink of water and head for her warm, comfy bed. But as she finished and turned off the light before heading to her room, in the darkness an arm circled her waist and pulled her close. From the scent of aftershave that filled the air she knew it was Mitch.

"Marry me, Tassie," he breathed into her ear. "I've loved you from the moment you set foot in my house. It just didn't feel right to admit it until we talked to Dale."

She swallowed hard then held her breath. Was she hallucinating? Had she been underwater too long? Her brain been deprived of its much needed oxygen?

"I know my proposal is unexpected and I have no right to ask you this soon," he went on, "and I wouldn't be surprised if you slapped me. I'm not asking because you saved my son's life—it's because I love you. I—I want to spend the rest of my life with you."

"Marry—you?" she squeaked out, still in shock.

"We've spent many hours together these past couple of months, you and I. We probably know one another better than many couples do after a long engagement. I know I don't have much to offer you, a worn-out cop who works long hours with kids who are enough to drive any sane woman away, but I—"

"But your kids would never want you to marry me! They hate me."

"I've finally realized it's not you they hate. Like Dale said, it would be the same for any woman who came into our home. They'll come around once they realize I love you. Look at Tony. He's bound to accept you after what you just did for him, and Babette's already crazy about you."

"You really think so?"

"I know so." His cheek lightly caressed hers.

"But what about Delana?"

"Where's your faith? If God wants us together, can't He change her mind, too? Look, Tassie dear, I don't have a mansion or unlimited funds to lavish upon you, and I'm not only a failure as a father but as a husband and as a Christian, as well, so I wouldn't blame you if you walked out that door come September and never looked back. But I can promise you one thing: If you say yes and marry me, I'll love you until death us do part and I'll try my best to be the God-fearing, God-serving, God-loving husband you deserve."

"I—I. . ."

"Shh, don't answer now. Before you say no, I want you to think about it. Like I said, I don't feel this way about you because you saved my son, and not because Babette loves you, and certainly not because of the wonderful way you keep this house and this family going, or the way you cook. I love you for you, sweet Tassie, and I want to love you as my wife." With that he gathered her in his arms and kissed her.

She thought she was going to melt right there in his arms from the sheer wisps of delight that coursed through her body. Mitch, the man who had been the center of her wishful dreams, was there in the darkness, holding her, kissing her, declaring his love.

Finally, when their lips parted and he released her, all she could do was sigh in contentment. Never had she been so happy and yet at the same time, so confused.

"See you in the morning, my love," he whispered and then he was gone, having disappeared into the darkness of the house.

Tassie felt as if her feet never touched the floor as she made her way to her room. After kicking off her shoes and preparing for bed, she picked up the phone and dialed a number. "Hi, Mom," she said, trying to keep her voice calm. "I know it's your bedtime, but I had to call you. I—I have good news. Mitch just asked me to marry him!"

"Tassie? Is—is that you? We must have a bad connection. I thought you said something about marriage."

"Yes, Mom, it's me, and I did say something about marriage. Mitch proposed to me!"

"Proposed to you? Why? You hardly know each other. Why would he do such a thing?"

"I know it sounds crazy, but I love him, Mom. I think I've loved him since the first day I came to work here. We've spent a lot of time together. He's never been anything but kind to me. He's a wonderful man. He—"

"Tassie, even if that were so and you two *were* in love, think about it. Do you really want to marry a man who already has three children? I know Mitch is good-looking and seems quite nice, but to marry him?"

She gazed at the third finger on her left hand, trying to imagine what it would be like to wear Mitch's wedding ring. "But, Mom, Mitch shares my faith and you know how important that is to me."

"But I thought you said he hadn't been attending church for several years before he started going with you."

"He hadn't been but he had accepted Christ as his Savior when he was a boy."

"I can't imagine a Christian not wanting to go to church."

"It wasn't that he didn't want to go. He's been so busy with work and his family, he's gotten away from the Lord. But he's a new man now, Mom. He's doing a turnaround. He wants to be close to the Lord. He loves going to church with me."

"Maybe he's just doing that to win you over. And what about his children? Wouldn't you rather have children of your own?"

Tassie searched her heart. "Of course I want children of my own, but I love Mitch's children." *Or at least I'm trying to.* "We could always have children if we decided we wanted more. And, Mom, you're wrong about him lying to me to win me over. You don't know him like I do. He'd never do that."

"He mustn't have been much of a husband to his first wife. Didn't you say she left him?"

"Yes. But she's the one who left, not Mitch. Left not only her husband but her three children. She couldn't have been much of a wife or mother to be able to walk away like that."

"Well, I'd certainly want to know more about their breakup before committing to him if I were you."

"I do know, Mom. He told me all about it."

"Oh, sweetheart, I don't know about this," her mother said with concern. "Take your time. Don't do something rash. You haven't told him yes already, have you?"

"No, but I want to. He told me to think about it."

"Smart man. I'll give him that much credit. Every girl should think long and hard before accepting a marriage proposal, but it's your life. You've always been levelheaded and made wise decisions. Whatever choice you make, I'm sure it will be the right one. But first pray about it. Let God lead you."

"Thanks, Mom. I didn't want to upset you, but I had to call you. I was so excited I was about to burst."

"I'm not upset, dear, just a little shocked. By the way, I called you this afternoon just to visit, but no one answered the phone."

"I drove Tony and his friends out to the lake."

"Oh? Did you swim? I know how you love the water."

Not wanting to go into detail, Tassie bit at her lip. "Sorta. I'll tell you all about it later. Good night, Mom. I love you. Don't forget to pray for me."

"I won't forget, sweetheart. I'm confident God will lead you to do whatever is in His perfect will as long as you remain open to it. I love you, too. Sweet dreams."

Totally worn-out after her unusual and busy day, Tassie yawned as she hung up the phone. *My dreams will be sweet, all right, and all about Mitch.*

&

Mitch was already dressed and waiting for her, drinking a cup of coffee at the table, when she entered the kitchen the next day. "Morning."

She grinned. "Good morning to you. You already made the coffee?"

After placing his cup on the table, he rose and sauntered over to her. "Yeah, I'll pour you a cup, but first. . ." He paused and gave her a bashful grin that made her heart sing. "First, I'd like to hold you in my arms and give you a good-morning kiss—if you'll let me."

Not sure how she should respond, Tassie simply stared at him.

"You're not upset with me, are you—about last night?"

She shook her head.

He extended his arms toward her then opened them wide. "Then come to me, Tassie."

His words were all it took. Without pondering his invitation or wondering if she should or should not, she leaped into his arms, lifted her face to his, and welcomed his kisses.

"Does this mean you'll marry me?" he asked when he finally allowed her to pull away.

"I think so, but I still need time, Mitch—just a few days. I won't take long. To me, as I'm sure it is to you, marriage is a lifetime commitment. We both need to pray about it. We want to be sure this is God's will for our lives."

Mitch dramatically wiped at his brow. "Whew, you scared me. There for a moment I thought you were going to say no, mainly because I'm still not sure you could ever love me."

"Ever love you? Mitch! I think I've loved you since the day I came to work for you!" Her words plummeted out before she could stop them. Not that she really wanted to stop them; she just hadn't planned on voicing them quite that way or at this moment.

He grabbed her up and whirled her about the room. "You do? You actually love me? Wow!"

"Of course, you silly! How else could I have put up with all the trauma you and your children have put me through?" she teased.

"I hate to admit it, but there may be more traumas in the future—before we get this thing licked."

"I know."

"And I want you to finish your education, Tassie. I'd never want marriage to me to stand in your way. I know how important it is to you."

"I've been thinking," she stated, grinning with a mischievousness lilt to her voice. "Maybe I should delay it for another year. Somehow, finishing my education doesn't seem nearly as important now as it did when you hired me." Her grin faded. "Mitch, if we do marry I want to be a full-time mother to your children, not just a caretaker. I don't mean as a replacement for their own mother but as a second mother, one who loves them as her own and wants them to love her. Is that asking too much?"

"Not at all. In fact, that is exactly what I had hoped you would do. My children need a mother figure in their life. Just look what you've accomplished with Babette. That child has done a complete turnaround."

"Babette is a beautiful child, Mitch. All she needed was love."

"Tony was already coming around, and after what you did for him yesterday, I have a feeling he, too, is going to change." He paused thoughtfully. "It's Delana I'm worried about. To be honest, I have no idea how she will respond if you accept my proposal."

"I know. Rather than make any headway with Delana, I'm afraid all I've done is cause more problems. If I do accept your proposal, please don't get me an engagement ring. Seeing me wearing your ring would upset her even more."

Mitch lovingly gazed into her eyes and stroked her cheek with his finger. "As much as I'd want you to wear my ring, I know you're right."

"I want so much to get along with your daughter. I wish she wasn't so angry all the time."

"Everything you've done, you've done to help her. I think her mother's leaving us for another man hit her much harder than I realized."

"Mitch, tell me about June. If I'm to even consider being your wife, I need to know everything. You said she left you for another man. Was that the only reason she left? Had you two been having marital problems?"

He lowered her to her feet and motioned toward a chair at the kitchen table. "Yeah, I guess you could say we'd always had marital problems. June's beauty, her free spirit, her carefree zest for life, her impulsiveness—all the things that had drawn me to her in the first place—became the things that separated us once we became husband and wife. She loved bragging to her friends that she was a cop's wife, but she hated that it took up so much of my time. She spent money—money we didn't have—without a thought to living on a budget but wouldn't even consider going to work to help pay for those things. I shouldn't be talking this way about her. I'm sure she had legitimate complaints about me, too."

"Yes, Mitch, you should. I need to know. Surely there was some love between the two of you during your married years. You had three children."

Rubbing his forehead, he began to pace about the kitchen. "I did love her, and I wanted to have children with her. She didn't. But her girlfriends were all having babies, so she decided she would, too. She loved being pregnant with Delana and strutting around in her maternity clothes, and she was a fairly good mother at first. Then Tony came along. Caring for two children was way more than she could handle."

"What about Babette?"

"June left me the first time several years before Babette was born. About a year later she appeared at the door and begged my forgiveness and I took her back. The next few months were like a second honeymoon—until the doctor told her she was pregnant again. She was determined to have an abortion but I told her if she did, it was all over between the two of us. From that day on, it was like I was her enemy. She couldn't say a civil word to me and she turned her back on Delana and Tony."

"But surely when she saw Babette's sweet little face and held her in her arms she—"

"No, she barely paid any attention to Babette, and she was

gone all the time. We went through babysitter after babysitter because she would never come home at the time she said she would. I tried to reason with her but she wouldn't listen."

Tassie reached out to him. "Oh, Mitch, how awful that must have been for all of you."

He sat down beside her and cradled her hand in his. "It was an awful time. It sounds mean-spirited for me to say it, but after finding out she'd been cheating behind my back with her lover again, I was almost glad when she left us that second time. I'm sorry to say it, but I'd had about all I could take—we all had; and after what she had done, I'd never have been able to trust her again."

"Mitch, I'm so sorry. I know it has been hard for you— telling me all of this—but knowing what you and the children have gone through gives me a better understanding of so many things. Not only of you, but of Tony's and Delana's attitudes, especially Delana's. Being the oldest she probably remembers more of what happened than the other children do."

"I'm sure she does, but sweetheart, we can't let her keep us apart. Delana is almost sixteen. In a few years, even if she doesn't go to college, she probably won't be living at home. Once most girls graduate from high school all they can think about is getting out on their own. I doubt Delana will be an exception."

"You're probably right. I love my parents dearly, and have always gotten along with them fabulously well, but I, too, wanted to get out on my own. Moving out of your parents' house is like announcing to the world you have arrived, that you are now an adult."

"And it seems to me the best thing I can do for her while she is still with me is to keep her under the influence of a positive, cheerful, godly woman. You, my love."

"She doesn't want my influence. She can barely stand the sight of me."

"I know. She doesn't want my influence, either. I won't try to deceive you by telling you it will be easy—I'm sure it won't. And I can't say she won't break your heart with her hateful words and her uncalled-for actions—because I'm sure that will happen." His shoulders rose and fell in a shrug. "I'm selfish for even asking you to share your life with my dysfunctional family."

"But I *want* to share my life with your family. I not only want to share it, I want to be an active and accepted part of it. I love your children, Mitch, and while I hate what she does and the way she behaves toward others—especially you and me—I love Delana because she is a part of you and because God loves her."

"Then you might say yes?"

"I want to say yes, but first I have something I must tell you, something that has been weighing on my mind for nearly ten years. Something I have to tell you before I accept your proposal."

Mitch raised a brow. "Uh-oh. That sounds ominous."

Tassie blinked hard. "I—I'm not the unblemished, squeaky clean person you think I am."

A frown clouded his face. "What do you mean?"

"It'll be easier to tell you if I start at the beginning." She pulled away from the shelter of his arms and began to pace about the room. "When I was a sophomore in high school one of the senior boys, the star quarterback on our football team, asked me for a date. I was afraid, since he was older than me, my parents wouldn't let me go, so I never told them. Rather than letting him pick me up at my house I asked him to meet me at the mall. I thought we were going to a movie, but instead, he took me to his friend's house where there was a party and a lot of drinking going on. I had never even tasted liquor before that night. But everyone was drinking. So, even though I knew it was wrong, trying to be like them, I drank, too. I really didn't like the stuff, but my date kept filling my glass, so I kept chugging it down. Next thing I knew, we were in his car and—"

"He raped you?"

Her heart thundered in her ears. She had never voiced her experience to another living soul, not even her mother and especially not her dad.

"I know it sounds crazy, but I'm really not sure. I was so drunk by that time I was totally out of it, but he said I went along willingly. And he told me to keep my mouth shut or he'd tell everyone in school what we did. After that night he never looked my way again, acted as if he didn't even know me."

Mitch gazed at her as if spellbound, as if he couldn't believe what he was hearing. "That's terrible. What did you do?"

Tassie had tried so hard to put that fateful night out of her mind and here she was reliving it again. Voicing that horrid experience was making her sick to her stomach and she wanted to throw up.

"What could I do?" she asked with a shrug. "Nothing, absolutely nothing. I wanted to tell my mother but I couldn't. She thought I was her perfect little girl. The knowledge of what I had done would destroy her. And I was so naive. I thought every time someone had intimate relations with a person they automatically became pregnant. For the next five months I lived in dread and fear. My grades went down. I was queasy all the time. I thought sure I was having a baby. Until I checked some books out of the library and read about a home pregnancy test and found out I wasn't. But I'll tell you one thing. I did a lot of praying. What I had done was sin and I knew it. Even though I didn't deserve forgiveness, I asked God to forgive me and dedicated my life to serving Him. I've been walking with Him ever since."

"Oh, Tassie, I wish I'd been there to protect you."

"I'm so ashamed of what I did, Mitch. I know God forgave me for my stupidity but He never promised I'd forget. That awful time in my life haunts me every day."

"What happened to the guy?"

She shrugged her shoulders sadly. "I have no idea, and I hope I never see him again. What happened to me is in the past. I want to keep it that way. God forgave me. That's the important thing." Her eyes filled with tears of shame. "If you've changed your mind and don't want to marry me, I'll understand."

Mitch leaped to his feet and gathered her up in his arms, holding her close. "Change my mind? Why would I want to do such a thing? You must have been about Delana's age. You thought you could trust the guy. He knew what he was doing when he plied you with alcohol."

"But I—"

He put a finger to her lips to silence her. "My dearest, like God's Word says, we've all sinned, every one of us, certainly me included. No one is less deserving of His forgiveness than I am, but He has promised to forgive us our sins if we but ask. You asked Him and He's forgiven you. How could I even begin to hold anything against you for being naive and becoming that man's victim?"

"You're not upset with me about it?"

"Of course not, sweetheart. I'm just thankful you came out of it as well as you did. Things could have been a lot worse. But, my dear Tassie, you need to forgive yourself."

"I know, and I'm going to. I can't believe I've been stupid enough to carry this burden for so long."

"Let's you and me forget about the whole thing and never speak of it again."

Tassie stood on tiptoe and kissed Mitch on the cheek. "I love you."

He gave her a shy grin. "I love you more, my darling. Just think, if you say yes, you'll be Mrs. Mitchell Drummond."

"Then, knowing this about me, you still want me to marry you?"

"Of course I do. I love you!"

Tassie gazed into the eyes of the only man she'd ever loved then threw her arms about his neck. "Then, yes, Mitch, my darling. Yes, yes, yes! I'll marry you!"

"Really? When?"

"Whenever you say. I want so much to be your wife. Oh, Mitch, this is so exciting. I love you. I love you. I love you!"

"What do you think about having the wedding at your church but having our friend, Dale Lewis, perform the ceremony instead of your pastor?"

"I think it's a wonderful idea."

"I've got to tell the kids!"

"You know they're going to be upset."

"But Dale said we should be honest with them. Besides, we can't wait too long, sweetheart. The college fall semester will be starting in a few weeks. I'd like for us to be married before then. How about two weeks from today?"

"Two weeks from today for what?" Delana asked as she entered the kitchen, her eyes narrowing suspiciously. "You hugging our servant because she saved your son, or is something else going on?"

Scowling, Mitch let go of Tassie and hurried toward his

daughter. "How many times do I have to remind you? Tassie is not our servant; she is our nanny. Tassie and I had decided we would tell you three children at the same time but since you're here and questioning our relationship, I guess you should be the first to know. I've asked her to marry me and she said yes."

Her eyes blazing, Delana glared at her father. "You're going to marry our maid? You've got to be kidding."

"Look, Delana, I love Tassie and I hope you will learn to love her, too. She's—"

"Love her? The way she treats me? Forget it, Dad! And don't count on me being at your wedding, 'cause I won't be there!" With that she turned and bolted out of the room. Moments later, she slammed her bedroom door hard enough to knock it off its hinges.

With a look of defeat, Mitch turned back to Tassie. "Now she's really upset."

"Don't beat yourself up. No matter when you told her it wouldn't have made any difference. She's determined to hate me."

He reached for her hands then gripped them tightly in his. "Her tirade hasn't made you change your mind, has it?"

"No, I still want to be your wife. Hopefully, with much prayer on our part, eventually she'll come around like Dale Lewis said she would and realize I want only the best for her."

He kissed her on the forehead then let his kisses slowly drift down her cheek to her lips. "So what do you think about having our wedding in two weeks?"

"It's a little fast, but I love the idea. Like you said, we probably know each other better than many couples do who have been dating for a long time. But I think a small wedding of just friends and family, and maybe those you have worked with over the years, would be best. Maybe if we keep it limited to just a few people, Delana will decide to come. A small wedding shouldn't take too much planning."

"But you will wear a white gown, won't you?"

"Oh, yes. This may be your second wedding, but it's my first."

They parted quickly as Tony and Babette came into the room. "Hey, what's going on with Delana? It felt like an earthquake when she slammed her door. She mad or somethin'?"

Mitch shot a quick glance at Tassie. "I guess now is as good a time as any to tell you. I've asked Tassie to marry me and she said yes!"

Tony grinned. "Now I know why Delana slammed her door."

Mitch did a double take. "You're not upset about it?"

"Naw, I knew you guys were getting along pretty well."

"Daddy, what does married mean?"

Mitch bent quickly and lifted Babette in his arms. "Oh, honey, I'm sorry. I should have done a better job of telling you kids. Married means Tassie won't be our nanny anymore, she—"

"But I want her to be my nanny. I love Tassie!" Babette began to cry.

Tassie quickly pulled the girl from Mitch's arms and held her close. "Oh, honey, I'm not leaving. I'll still be living here and taking care of you. Things will just be a little bit different."

"I guess that means you'll be our mom," Tony said matter-of-factly.

She whirled around to face him. "No, Tony! No one can ever take your mother's place, but I would like to be like a second mom to you. I love you kids."

"So when is the wedding?"

"Two weeks," Mitch said proudly. "In two weeks Tassie will be Mrs. Mitchell Drummond."

❧

"Since it's a warm day, I thought we'd pick up some chocolate chip ice cream," Tassie told Babette the next afternoon after they had visited the library and she pulled the car into the grocery store's parking lot. "Would you like that?"

Babette's eyes sparkled. "Yummy. I love ice cream."

"Me, too."

"I like going to the store with you, Tassie."

"And I like going to the store with you!"

They purchased their ice cream then headed for home, only to be surprised when they saw Dale Lewis coming out their front door with Delana a few steps behind him. *Oh, please, God, don't let Delana be in any trouble,* Tassie breathed in prayer as she pulled in beside them. But Dale was smiling. That had to be good sign.

"Hi," he told her with a friendly wave. "I saw Delana walking home from the mall, so I stopped to give her a ride."

When Tassie turned to smile at Delana she found the girl's mascara smeared, as if she had been crying. "You could have called me, Delana. I would have been happy to pick you up."

Dale grinned. "Naw, it worked out better this way. It gave me and Delana a chance to have a chat. Gotta go. See you all later."

Tassie watched until his car disappeared down the street. When she turned around, Delana had already gone back into the house.

"Did either of them say what they chatted about?" Mitch asked her after he got home. "Did she seem mad at him or upset?"

"If she would have been mad at him, I doubt she would have walked him to his car, but she did sort of look like she had been crying. Maybe you should ask him."

He shrugged. "I know it sounds silly, but I'm not real sure he'd tell me. He's pretty tight-lipped when it comes to counseling someone."

Her eyes widened. "You think that's what he was doing? Counseling her?"

Again he shrugged. "Who knows? Maybe. I doubt Delana will tell us and if I ask her she'll probably get mad and tell me it's none of my business. I guess if he did counsel her, we'll have to pray she pays attention to him. I know it won't be easy, but let's try to put all this out of our minds for now and think of something pleasant. We have a wedding to plan."

Tassie gazed lovingly into his eyes. "I need to talk to you about something."

"Oh no. Don't tell me you've changed your mind about marrying me."

"Oh, no, nothing like that, but I've been thinking. Now that we're engaged and I'm no longer simply an employee in your house, it seems improper for us to be living under the same roof."

"But I need you with the kids."

"I know, and I have a plan. I was thinking I could move back to my parents' home and come to work every morning at six to prepare breakfast and be here with the kids all day. Then I'd leave as soon as Babette goes to bed and—"

"But what if I get home late or am called out during the night?"

"I haven't asked Mom yet, but I think she would be willing to come and spend the nights at your house until we're married."

Mitch wrinkled up his face. "That seems kinda silly."

"Maybe, but I think it would set a good example for the children."

"I'm sure you're right. As Christians we don't want any appearance of impropriety."

"Good, I was hoping you'd agree with me. I'll call Mom in the morning."

❧

Although the next few days were filled with a flurry of activity and more happiness than Tassie had ever before experienced, there was still a constant strain between Tassie and Delana. It wasn't that the girl was rude or said or did anything out of the ordinary; instead it was as if a heavy gray cloud hung between them.

"Delana, dear, I wish you wouldn't treat Tassie the way you do," Tassie overheard her mother saying in a sweet voice. "Tassie loves you."

Tassie's mother had stayed at the house this morning to help with some final details, and Tassie—just coming out of the kitchen—stopped short, not wanting to interrupt.

The girl responded with a loud huff. "Loves me? If she loves me why is she so mean to me?"

"Come on now, sweetheart. What has my daughter ever done to you that was mean?"

"She's always messing in my stuff and spying on me."

"It may seem that way to you but all she's doing is trying to help you."

"I don't need her help. I just want to be left alone."

"Please, Delana," Mrs. Springer pleaded with her, "this isn't just Tassie's wedding; it's your father's, too. He loves you, and despite what you may believe, we all love you. Nothing would make him any happier than to have you attend their wedding.

Promise you'll think long and hard before doing something foolish enough to break his heart."

Delana huffed. "His heart is already broken. My mom took care of that a long time ago."

"Believe me, Tassie isn't going to run out on you, sweetie. She isn't just marrying your father, she's marrying his family. She wants so much to be a second mother to you kids. And. . ."

When she paused, Tassie backed away a bit.

"And she wants so much for you to be her maid of honor."

"Her maid of honor? No way!"

Tassie listened as a noise sounded, like a plastic bag tearing or a box being pulled open.

"Look, I've brought her prom dress," her mother said kindly. "It's your size. I know it will fit you."

"Since I'm not going to the wedding, I won't be needing it."

"I'll leave it here, in case you change your mind. You'd look so pretty in pink. Just imagine how happy your father would be if you walked up that aisle toward him, wearing that dress."

As the two moved toward the doorway, Tassie rushed back into the kitchen, lest she be discovered. *Oh, Mom, if anyone can reach Delana it will be you with your sweet spirit. If only I were more like you.*

⁂

Despite Delana's absence, the dinner and wedding rehearsal went well that evening. Tassie was glad Mitch had asked Chaplain Lewis to perform their ceremony. She liked him. He was one of the strongest Christians she had ever met and just the kind of man Mitch needed at this time of his life. His wise counseling was exactly what they'd both needed.

Although both Tassie and Mitch were concerned about his daughter's reluctance to attend their wedding, once they reached home they spent a pleasant hour holding hands and cuddling on the sofa, declaring their love for one another.

About eleven, she gave Mitch a final kiss and hug then excused herself, with plans to go to her parents' home and get a good night's sleep.

੨ፅ

The ringing of her cell phone wakened Tassie a little before two. After flipping on the light she answered with a sleepy, "Hullo," but the sobs and the upset voice she heard in response made her eyes open wide and her heart quiver with fear.

eleven

"Tassie, I need your help."

Tassie gripped the phone tighter. "Delana?" There was a pause but she could still hear sobbing.

"I've done something terrible." The words came out between sniffles.

Tassie sat straight up in bed. "Where are you? It's after midnight. I thought you'd be in bed by now!"

"I—I snuck out my window and climbed down the tree right after my dad went to bed."

"Why? Why would you do such a thing and where are you? I hear music."

"At the Wal-Mart store over on Locust."

"What are you doing there?"

"I don't want to call my dad. Can you come and get me?"

Tassie glanced at the clock. "Of course I can, but why can't you call your father?"

"Just come, please," the anxious voice pleaded amid sobs.

Tassie glanced at the clock again. "You still haven't told me what you're doing at Wal-Mart this time of night."

"I'll tell you when you get here, I promise."

"Wait for me inside, by the customer service counter. Don't, under any circumstances, go outside until I get there, you hear me?"

"Okay, but please hurry!"

Tassie's heart pounded in her ears as loud as a kettledrum as she hurriedly slipped into her jeans and T-shirt and headed for the Wal-Mart store.

But when she reached the store, before entering, she paused long enough to dial a familiar number on her cell phone.

When she finally made her way through the big glass doors she found Delana waiting right where she had told her. Wrapping an arm about the girl she led her toward her car. Once they were safely inside with the door locks engaged, she turned to her with a look of concern. "Delana, please tell me why you were here instead of at home in bed. I need to know."

Delana wiped at her heavily mascaraed eyes and swallowed hard. "I was mad at Daddy for getting married, so I decided to run away from home. My boyfriend was going to go with me, but neither of us had a car—so—I took Daddy's keys off of the hall table after he went downstairs and—"

"You took your Dad's car?"

"No, I took the minivan. I had to have it to run away."

"What did you plan to do for money? Gas is expensive and you'd have to eat and have a place to stay."

The girl hung her head. "I took Daddy's billfold and his credit cards. I took the money from his desk, too."

"How much was that?"

"About a thousand dollars."

"You knew your dad was saving that money for emergencies. If you and your boyfriend were running away and you had the minivan and that money, why did you call me?" She glanced around the parking lot. "By the way, where is he?" *And the minivan.*

"He got scared when I wrecked the—"

"You wrecked the van?"

"I couldn't help it, Tassie. Some guy stopped real quick in front of me, and I ran off the road to keep from hitting him!"

"Were either of you hurt?"

"Not really, just shook-up a bit, but it scared me really bad. We ended up in a deep ditch about four blocks from here."

"Did you call the police and report your accident?"

"No. I was afraid they'd call Daddy."

"You mean the minivan is still there?"

"Yes. I sorta hit a tree."

"Oh, my." Tassie rubbed her forehead. "You're going to have to tell him what happened, you know. We can't just let the van stay down in that ditch overnight. When did your boyfriend leave you?"

Delana winced at the question. "Right after it happened."

"Just took off and left you?"

She nodded.

"And you walked to Wal-Mart by yourself? It would have been much safer if you'd locked yourself in the car. Why didn't you call me then instead of risking your life by walking alone in the dark?"

"Because I was afraid you'd call Daddy."

Stricken with fear over what might have happened to the girl, Tassie reached across and placed her hand on Delana's arm. "God must have had His hand of protection on you, Delana; otherwise some guy might have come along and tried to get you into his car."

Delana covered her face with her hands. "A man in a car did offer me a ride, but I told him no."

Tassie scooted closer and gathered the quivering girl in her arms. "But he didn't try to get you into the car?"

"No, he just drove off. Daddy's going to kill me for taking the minivan and his money. I hated to call you, but I was afraid to call him"

She stroked the girl's hair. "Didn't I tell you I'd be there for you if you ever needed me?"

"Yes, but I've done some things—"

"The things you've done have upset me but they didn't keep me from loving you. But I still don't understand why you would try to run away, especially without leaving a note so your father wouldn't worry about you."

"I—I didn't think he'd care that I was gone. Even though Mr. Lewis said he did, I never thought my dad loved me. He's never treated me as nice as he treats you."

"Oh, honey, he's always loved you. You're his daughter. Besides, the love your dad and I share is a totally different kind of love than the love he has for you. You're his baby, his Delana." Tassie gently ran a finger down the girl's cheek. "No one could ever take your place in his heart, not me, not anyone. It's important that you know that. Oh, sweetie, I'm so sorry you felt that way. No matter what you do, your father will always love you. You're his flesh and blood. His precious child."

"I guess what I did *was* pretty stupid."

"Yes, it was, but you're not the first girl to do something really dumb. I—"

Both Tassie and Delana startled as a rap sounded on the girl's window and Mitch's face appeared.

Delana swung around angrily as Tassie hurriedly lifted the door's lock to allow him entrance. "You called him?"

"I had to, sweetie. He's your father. He deserved to know."

"What's going on, and why are you at Wal-Mart this time of night?" Mitch asked, an angry tinge to his voice.

Delana dipped her head and cowered beneath his penetrating gaze. "I'm sorry, Daddy, but as much trouble as I've caused you, I thought you'd be glad I was gone," she explained between sobs.

"Gone? What do you mean *gone*?"

"I—I was running away."

"Running away? How could you even think of running away?"

When she sent a glance for help toward Tassie, Tassie answered for her. "She took the minivan, Mitch."

"Delana, how could you?" Mitch glanced around the parking lot. "Surely you weren't running away alone. Was someone else with you? Where is the minivan?"

Again, Delana winced. "My boyfriend was going with me but he got scared when I . . ."

His eyes widened. "When you what?"

"It wasn't my fault, Daddy. Someone made me run off the road!"

"You had a wreck?" He gave her a frantic once-over. "Are you okay?"

"Uh-huh, I'm okay but—but the minivan is in a ditch."

"About four blocks from here," Tassie inserted then watched with a broken heart as Mitch, a big, strong man who had faced many a hardened criminal, buried his face in his daughter's hair and began to weep.

"Where is your boyfriend? Was he hurt?"

"He left right after the accident happened. I—I guess he went back home."

A scowl dented Mitch's forehead. "Good thing. If I had him here I'd want to wring his neck. Was this running away thing his idea or yours?"

Tassie grabbed hold of Mitch's wrist. "The important thing is that Delana is safe and uninjured."

He stared at his daughter for a moment then wrapped his arms around her. "Tassie's right. I love you, Delana, you have to believe that. I don't know what I would have done if anything had happened to you. You and your brother and sister are the most important things in my life. Without the three of you, life wouldn't be worth living. You three and Tassie *are* my life!"

"But, Daddy, how can you say that? You're never home, and when you are—you're always yelling at me."

"I know and I'm sorry, Delana, so sorry. I've been a terrible father to you three kids. It nearly killed me when your mother left. I guess I never fully realized how much it hurt you, too. Instead of worrying about how her leaving affected you kids, I wallowed in my own self-pity. I guess I tried to forget about her and the rejection *I* felt by throwing myself into my work. How can I even begin to ask you to forgive me? If I had been the father I should have been, you wouldn't have felt the need to run away from me."

"I'm sorry, Daddy. I didn't mean to scare you."

Mitch pulled her close, sheltering her in his arms. "Please, baby, promise me you won't leave me again."

"I won't. I promise." Pressing her face into his chest, Delana sobbed like a baby.

Tears trailed down Tassie's cheeks as she watched the scene playing out before her. It was a tender moment she would never forget.

Mitch planted a kiss on his daughter's forehead then lifted her face to his. "I've been a miserable example to you children, but I'm trying to change. I want us to be a real family, Delana, the kind of family God intended us to be, and you are such an important part of it." He let out a sigh that seemed to come from the pit of his stomach. "I should have taken you children to church when you were little, even though your mom refused to go."

"You're taking us now."

"And I plan to continue taking you, but we can talk about

that later. Right now, Tassie needs to head back to her mother's house and I want you to show me where the minivan is so I can call a wrecker."

❧

The fact that the house was quiet the next morning when Tassie entered didn't surprise her. The children were being allowed to sleep late since they were on summer break. She found Mitch and her mother sitting at the kitchen table, engaged in conversation.

"Morning, sweetheart." Mitch rose, kissed her cheek, and pulled out a chair for her. "Sit down. I'll pour you a cup of coffee."

She thanked him then glanced toward her mother. "I guess Mitch told you what happened last night after you'd gone to bed."

"Yes, he did. It must have been a pretty harrowing experience for all of you. I'm sorry I didn't hear Delana leave. Maybe if I had, this whole thing could have been avoided."

Tassie hurriedly gave her mother's hand a pat. "Don't blame yourself, Mom. You couldn't possibly have heard her from where you were sleeping in my room above the garage. Besides, she knew her father was downstairs in his room. I'm sure she went out of her way to be quiet."

Mitch placed Tassie's cup of coffee on the table then nodded in agreement as he sat down beside her. "She's right, Mrs. Springer, and you couldn't have stopped her even if you'd tried. There is no one to blame for this fiasco but me."

Tassie quickly leaned toward him and cupped his hand in hers. "Don't be so hard on yourself. She's talked about running away several times, but neither of us ever thought she would go through with it."

"I sure didn't. I figured her threats were nothing more than a means of getting her way."

"Whatever her reason, at least she's home now and not off in some stranger's hands who could do her harm."

"Yes, praise the Lord for watching over her." He gave Tassie a half smile. "I'm glad, since she was afraid to call me, she called you. I wouldn't have handled things nearly as well."

Tassie swallowed at the lump that had suddenly risen in her throat. "I was afraid she'd be furious with me for calling you, but once she realized you weren't going to be too angry with her, she seemed to have forgotten it."

Scooting his chair even closer, he wrapped his arm about her shoulders. "You did the right thing, sweetheart; you had to let me know. Surely, she realized you had no choice but to call me."

"Mitch is right," her mother offered. "I'm sure Delana is glad you called her father. Once that boyfriend of hers took off and left her alone, she knew she was in trouble and the only people who could help her were the ones who loved her. And she did tell Mitch she was sorry. Shower her with love and understanding, give her a little time and space, pray for her like you've never prayed for her before, and let God handle things. After all, isn't He the God of love?"

Tassie blinked back tears, tears of love and appreciation for her mother and her valuable insight. "Thanks, Mom. You always have the right answer."

"I agree." Mitch smiled at Tassie. "I'm sure glad I'm marrying a woman with such a smart mom."

A sweet expression blanketed Mrs. Springer's countenance. "And I'm glad my daughter is marrying a man who is big enough to admit his mistakes, and with God's leading, willing to work to make changes." She rose, and after placing her cup in the dishwasher, turned to face them. "Now if you'll excuse me, I'll leave you two lovebirds alone and go home to my husband. I'll see you both at the church."

Once they heard the front door close, Mitch pulled Tassie close and leaned his head against hers. "Know what day this is?"

She gave him a coy smile. "Friday?"

"Yeah, Friday, but that's not what I mean."

She pursed her lips thoughtfully. "Umm, it isn't a special holiday, is it?"

"It is for me. I'm getting married today."

She lifted her face toward his with a mischievous smile. "You're getting married? And you didn't invite me to your wedding? I don't remember receiving an invitation."

He playfully brushed his lips across hers. "I'm inviting you now. Not only to come to my wedding but to spend the rest of your life with me."

She pulled away and glanced up at him. "Your life? Oh, my. What will your new bride think about that?"

"Since you, my beloved Tassie, are the new bride I will be marrying in a few hours, I'm hoping you'll be as excited about spending the rest of your life with me as I am about spending my life with you." He lovingly stroked her hair. "This is the best day of my life."

"It's my very best day, too. I'm marrying the man I love and I'm gaining three wonderful children."

He tossed his head back with a laugh. "*Wonderful* children? I wouldn't exactly call them wonderful, considering all the mean, hateful things they've done to you. And surely you're not forgetting that because of Tony's reckless behavior you had to jump in the lake and save his life. And what about having to rescue Delana?"

"But, Mitch, don't you see? At the time those things seemed like terrible experiences, but I think God is using them for good. Tony and I have are finally becoming friends and Delana set her pride aside and called *me*, of all people, to come after her. I just know that, eventually, she will accept me. And hopefully she'll accept God, too."

He grinned. "You know, you're absolutely right. I hadn't thought of it that way. God does work in mysterious ways, His wonders to perform." He pulled her close again. "So does that mean you still want to go through with this wedding?"

"Yes, my love, more than ever." Tassie stood and kissed Mitch on the cheek. "I love you."

His lips tilted up in a smile. "I love you more, my darling. Tonight, you'll be Mrs. Mitchell Drummond."

She wrapped her arms about his neck and lovingly gazed into his eyes as she twined her fingers through his hair. "I know, and I can hardly wait."

"I know we haven't had much of a courtship, and I'm not a man of flowery words or a man of means, but I promise to spend the rest of my life doing everything I can to make you happy."

Lifting her hands she cupped his face between her palms. "And I love you, my precious one. You're the man of my dreams in every way."

He harrumphed. "Man of your dreams? A father with children who have given you more grief than any person should have to endure in a lifetime?"

"But, Mitch, once we say 'I do,' those children will become my children as well. I will share equally in the responsibility of bringing them up to be caring, productive, God-loving adults, a responsibility I gladly and joyfully accept."

The smile he gave her touched her heart. "You're crazy; you know that, don't you?"

She nodded. "Crazy about you! Oh, Mitch, I can hardly

wait to be your wife."

"And I'll be the proudest man alive." After nuzzling his chin in her hair, he bent and kissed her with a kiss that made her heart thunder and her head reel.

When they finally parted, he backed away. "I hate to leave you but I'd better get out of here. I know you have a million things to do before our wedding and so do I."

Her lower lip took on a pout. "You mean I won't see you again until our wedding?"

Smiling, he shrugged. "I guess not, unless you want to slip off and have lunch with me."

She snickered. "Is that an invitation?"

"Sure."

"At that little Italian place in the strip mall down the street?"

"If that's where you want to go."

"At straight up noon?"

"Yep, straight up noon."

"I'll be there. Mom is coming over in a few minutes. I'm sure she won't mind staying with the children until I get back."

She giggled like a schoolgirl. "See you at noon, my love!"

The rest of morning flew by as Tassie worked on countless tasks she was determined to complete before leaving for their wedding.

By eleven forty-five, when she left to meet Mitch for lunch, Delana still hadn't come out of her room.

"How's the lasagna?" he asked as they sat in a corner table in the little Italian restaurant, fondly gazing across the table at one another.

"It's wonderful but I'm too nervous to eat," she confessed, her mind still on Delana.

"You're still worried about her, aren't you?"

She nodded.

"I'm worried about Delana, too, sweetheart. But this is our day, Tassie. We can't let her ruin what should be the happiest day of our life."

She blinked at a tear. "I know but I so want her at our wedding and I know you do, too."

He reached across the table and took both her hands in his. "She knows it, too, sweetheart. We've got to leave it in God's hands."

"I'm trying. I not only wanted her to be there, I wanted her to be my maid of honor. I know I could have asked one of the ladies at the church, but if I can't have Delana I don't want anyone."

Mitch's thumb rubbed at her ring finger. "I wish I'd gotten you an engagement ring."

She gave her head a vigorous shake. "No, Mitch, an engagement ring on my finger would have only added to Delana's anger."

"Well, like it or not, as my wife you are going to wear a wedding ring." His expression softened as he gazed into her eyes. "A quite pretty wedding ring, if I do say so myself."

"Oh, Mitch, I hope you didn't spend more than you should have. A simple gold band is all I need."

They discussed the minor redecorating they planned to do to the house, the shrubs they wanted to plant in the front yard, and several other non-children subjects, then walked to their cars holding hands.

"You *will* show up at the church, won't you?" Mitch teased as he closed her car door and leaned into the open window.

She turned the key in the ignition then grinned up at him. "Absolutely. No way am I going to miss a chance to become Mrs. Mitchell Drummond." After blowing him a kiss, with a little wave she drove away.

ta

Delana was standing in the middle of the living room when Tassie entered the house. "I've been waiting for you. Your mom said you wanted to ask me something. I hope it's not about that bridesmaid thing."

"Sweetheart, I really want you to be my maid of honor at our wedding. Won't you please reconsider?"

Delana quirked up her face. "Why would you want me to be your maid of honor?"

"Because I love you, Delana. Mom said she showed you my prom dress. It may not be the kind of dress you'd pick to wear, but I'm sure it will fit you. We can even take the bow off. And your father and I both so want you at our wedding."

"I haven't even decided yet if I'm going."

Tassie reached for Delana's hand and was pleased when she didn't pull away. "Look, sweetie, I understand where you're coming from. With the exception of your father, the people you have loved the most are the ones who let you down and walked out of your life." She paused and with her free hand lifted the girl's face to meet hers. "I promise you on my word of honor, my precious Delana, I will never leave you. I'm here to stay. I've told you several times I wanted to be your friend and I still do. But more than that, I want us to share our lives together much like a mother and her natural daughter would. I want to be there proudly watching you when you graduate high school and when you walk down the aisle and pledge your life to the wonderful man you will one day meet and marry. I want to be there when you have children and be a grandmother to them. I want to share in your joys and sorrows, to be there for you whenever and wherever you need me. And most importantly, I want you to let me love you and for you to love me. I know it will take time but. . ." She stopped midsentence when tears began to trickle down Delana's cheeks.

"You're not just saying those things so I won't be mad about you marrying my dad?"

"Oh, honey, no! I mean every word! I can't tell you how much I want you there. Your father does, too!"

"Then—I guess I'll go."

"To our wedding?" Tassie felt her eyes widen. This was almost too good to be true.

"Yes, but I don't want to be your bridesmaid or whatever you called it."

"I'd really like to have you as my maid of honor but just knowing you will be at our wedding is a wonderful answer to prayer." Cautiously wrapping her arms about the girl, Tassie couldn't help but sob. God was answering her prayer, their prayer.

"Couldn't you get one of your friends at church to be your maid of honor?"

She shook her head. "No. I told your father if I couldn't have you I didn't want anyone."

Delana gazed up at her. "You really said that?"

"Yes, and I meant every word. I want you, sweetie. Only you. No one else."

"So if I don't do it you won't have one?"

"That's right."

The girl gave her a sheepish grin. "Then I guess I'll do it."

Tassie's heart nearly exploded with joy. "You will? Really?"

"Yeah, I guess so." She paused with a grin. "If your dress doesn't make me look stupid."

She glanced at her watch. "We still have a couple of hours. If you don't like it we'll make a quick run to the bridal shop. I can hardly wait to tell your dad! He'll be so pleased."

Delana shook her head. "No, don't. I want to surprise him."

"You mean we should keep it from him until he sees you come up the aisle?"

She nodded. "Yes. I think he'd like to be surprised."

After planting a quick kiss on the girl's cheek, she smiled. "Let's go take a look at that dress to see if it will work."

Delana smiled back. "I've already tried it on. If you take that stupid big bow off the back it will do just fine. In fact, I kinda liked it."

As the two ascended the stairs arm in arm, Tassie lifted her eyes heavenward. *Oh, God, my Father, how could I have doubted You?*

twelve

Mitch smiled at Dale Lewis as the two stood at the altar. "Surely you didn't wear that gun to our wedding."

Dale patted his coat. "Of course I did. Didn't I tell you and Tassie that gun goes with me everywhere I go?"

"This isn't a shotgun wedding," he responded with a grin. "No one is forcing me to marry this little gal. I'm doing it quite willingly."

Dale laughed, then his face sobered. "All kidding aside, Mitch, I hope you'll both remember the things the three of us talked about before the wedding rehearsal. Blending families is a tough job. You're going to have some rough times ahead, but God is faithful. He'll never fail you, and don't you fail Him. Take any differences you have to the Lord and leave them there for Him to handle and all will be well with you."

"I will, Dale. I've learned a lot these past three months. I won't make the same mistakes again; I promise."

"Just remember, I'm always here any time you need to talk."

"I will, old friend, and thanks."

He glanced toward Tony, who had agreed to be his best man, next at the doors at the back of the sanctuary, then at his watch. In a few minutes his bride would be coming through those doors.

He'd no more than had the thought when the organ began to play, the double doors opened, and their flower girl appeared—his adorable daughter, Babette, wearing the pretty pink dress Tassie had picked out for her. And her lips were turned up in a cute little smile that made his heart sing as she began to drop rose petals from her basket onto the floor.

Mitch felt as if he were going to explode with happiness. The only thing that could have made this day any better was if his oldest daughter would have agreed to attend the wedding instead of staying home by herself. But, to his joy, Tony and Babette were not only there, Tony had agreed to be his best man. At least that part of his and Tassie's prayers had been answered. Hopefully, now that they were being married, and since Tassie had been willing to rush to Delana's aid when she had needed her, the girl would begin to accept her as his new wife and give up on her crusade to get rid of her. *God,* he said in his heart, *if You could bring Tony and Babette around, then there has to be hope for Delana.*

❧

Tassie's mother dabbed at her eyes with her hanky as she stood in the bride's room off the sanctuary, smiling at her. "You've never looked more beautiful, my precious daughter. You make a lovely bride. I knew that dress was the perfect one for you the moment we saw it in that bridal shop window."

"I just hope Mitch likes it."

Her mother sent her an adoring smile. "How could he not like it?"

Tassie checked to make sure the little diamond stud earrings were in place—the something old she had borrowed from her mother. "You are happy for me, aren't you?"

"Oh, yes. Staying nights in Mitch's home to be with his children has made me see why you love him. He's a fine man, Tassie. He's made mistakes but he honestly loves his kids and wants to do the right thing. He's determined to make sure they have a Christian upbringing, and with you there to help him, I'll know he'll succeed."

Mrs. Springer turned to Delana. "You look pretty, too, young lady. That dress fits you like it was made for you. And your hair looks beautiful pulled up that way."

Delana fingered one of the long tendrils falling softly at her neckline. "Tassie did it."

"I'm so glad you decided to be Tassie's maid of honor, dear."

Delana smiled at Mrs. Springer then at Tassie. "I'm glad, too."

A chill coursed through Tassie as she gazed at Mitch's daughter. She hadn't won her to the Lord yet, but by showering the girl with love and prayer, she knew it would happen. "Your father is going to be so proud," she told her as she lovingly cradled the girl's cheek in her palm. "Now each one of his children—our children—will be taking part in our wedding. What a blessing!"

Tassie's dad grinned at the three as he pushed open the door a crack and pointed to the clock on the wall. "You ladies about ready? The groom and the best man are gettin' a little antsy out there waiting for you."

"Oh, my! I should be in my seat." Her mother shook a cautioning finger at both Tassie and Delana. "Remember, you girls, step, together, step, together, step, together. I know you're both going to be in a hurry to get to Mitch but take your time. Enjoy every moment of your walk up that aisle." She blew an air kiss toward her daughter. "Especially you, my baby girl. This is your wedding day, the day every girl dreams of. Make it special."

Tassie leaned forward and placed a gentle, loving kiss on her mother's cheek. "I will, Mom. I'm going to remember this day forever." She smiled toward Delana. "And having Delana here with me is truly making this day special."

Mrs. Springer motioned at Delana as she opened the door and the organ music sounded. "There's your cue. You'd better come with me. It's time for you to make your appearance."

With a final glance at Tassie, Delana followed her step-grandmother-to-be out the door.

"You're beautiful," Tassie's father told her when her mother and Delana had gone and they headed down the hall toward the sanctuary. "I can't tell you how proud I am of you. You've grown into a lovely young woman. You're going to make a wonderful wife."

Her emotions suddenly taking over, Tassie felt like crying. "I want to be a good wife, Daddy, and a good mother to his children. I so want Delana to give her life to God."

"Don't you worry about that girl. She's come a long way in the past twenty-four hours. With all of us praying for her, I have a feeling she'll soon be accepting our Lord. She's young and she's been hurt. Being rejected by her mother like she was had to have left deep scars. They take time to heal. But God is still our Great Physician and always will be. Healing that girl's heart is child's play for Him. Have faith, sweetheart. God is able and He wants to answer your prayer."

"Thanks, Daddy. You always know the right thing to say."

Taking hold of Tassie's hand, he slipped it into the crook of his arm. "Ready?"

She smiled up at him through tears of joy. "Oh, yes, Daddy. I'm ready!"

❧

As Babette reached the front of the church, Mitch glanced back toward the double doors. *Hurry, my love, please hurry.*

But the next person to enter wasn't Tassie; it was someone else. Had she asked one of the young women at the church to be her maid of honor and forgotten to tell him? He narrowed his eyes for a better look. *No, it can't be!*

But it was. It was Delana! Delana was here! Delana had

come to their wedding after all—and she was Tassie's maid of honor! *Oh, Father God, how good You are!*

Mitch's heart nearly melted when his daughter drew nearer—a vision of loveliness in a pink gown, her hair all piled on top her head—and she was wearing so little makeup he could barely see it. *God, You did this for me? When I'm so unworthy? I don't know how You did it but I praise You for it. You are truly an awesome God. Thank You! Thank You! Thank You!*

"I love you, my darling daughter," Mitch whispered to her when she reached the altar as he drew her into his arms and hugged her close.

"I love you, too, Daddy."

All rose as the strains of the wedding march filled the sanctuary and Tassie appeared in her glorious gown of white. Her eyes sparkled as she walked slowly toward the front of the sanctuary, pausing only long enough beside the front pew to present a single red rose to her mother.

"Who gives this woman in marriage to this man?" Chaplain Dale asked as she and her father stepped before him at the altar.

"Her mother and I do."

Tassie smiled as her dad kissed her cheek then placed her hand into Mitch's before turning to take his place by her mother.

"You're here! You're actually here and you're going to be my wife! And all three of my children are here. Is God good or what?" Mitch whispered as she stepped up beside him.

"Dearly beloved," Chaplain Dale began in his deep, rich voice. "We are gathered today to bear witness as this man and this woman are joined in the holy state of matrimony. Their marriage is being entered into with reverence. For there is no greater joy than for two like-minded souls who love each other and love God to be joined together. To strengthen each other in all ways, to support each other through all sorrow, and to share with each other in the gladness of life."

Mitch cast an adoring glance at Tassie and then at the beautiful young woman at her side.

"Marriage in itself is an act of faith," Dale continued, "an ever-deepening commitment. It is a loving union between a man and a woman. Marriage between two people who love one another has been described as the very best and most important relationship two people can share. Marriage was ordained by God Himself and it should never be entered into lightly. The apostle Paul compared the relationship between husband and wife to that between Christ and the church. Marriage is a decision of two individuals to share the same type of pure, Christian love described by Paul."

Although Mitch listened carefully to Chaplain Dale's words, he couldn't help thinking about God's miraculous answer to prayer.

"Mitch, Tassie, would you please hold hands and face one another?"

Tassie handed her bouquet to Delana then turned to Mitch. He eagerly took hold of both her hands. They felt warm, soft to the touch. Just holding her hands sent chills through his body.

"Mitch, repeat after me." Dale paused. "I take you, Tassie Springer, as my wife. To laugh with in joy, to grieve with in sorrow, and to grow more in love with each day as we serve God together."

His heart thundering against his chest, Mitch repeated the words with great sincerity and dedication. Loving Tassie was going to be the easy part. Being worthy of her love was what worried him.

"Now, Tassie, repeat after me." Again, Dale paused. "I take

you, Mitchell Drummond, as my husband. To laugh with in joy, to grieve with in sorrow, and to grow more in love with each day as we serve God together."

Mitch couldn't remember a more happy time in his life as he listened to Tassie repeat her vows.

"And I know you both intend to keep your vows. Trust each other and trust God and all will be well with you." Turning to Tony, Dale asked, "Do you have the rings?"

His lips tilted upward in a nervous grin, Tony reached into his pocket and pulled out two rings.

Mitch took the one with the small diamond solitaire and lovingly placed it on Tassie's finger. "This, my love, is a small token to remind you of my love and the pledge I've made to you this day."

The look of adoration on his beloved's face was almost more than he could bear. Although he had loved his first wife, the love he felt for Tassie was nothing like that love. This love felt permanent, fulfilling, satisfying, and, yes, challenging. With God's help he would do everything in his power to be the husband she deserved.

For a moment, Tassie gazed at the ring he'd placed on her finger then took the other ring from Tony and slipped it onto Mitch's finger.

"This ring, my precious one, is a small token of my love. May it symbolize the unending love I have for you. I commit my life to you, Mitch. May our love last a lifetime and may God grant us many years together as husband and wife."

Dale nodded toward Mitch. "You may kiss your bride."

Without a moment's hesitation, wrapping Tassie tightly in his arms, he complied.

❧

Tassie felt giddy with happiness as Mitch's lips pressed against hers. Never in her wildest dreams the day she quit her job and decided to move back to Grand Island did she imagine she would be marrying a wonderful man like Mitch and become the stepmother of three children. How good God had been to her, and she knew He would be good to her in the future as she took on the daunting task ahead of her and worked to deserve the love of his children.

"Let us pray." The chaplain bowed his head. "Oh eternal God, You have heard the words of promise these two have just spoken. May the Holy Spirit speak to this man and this woman and give them a sense of the sacred and binding power of their vows. May they be a blessing to each other, and to those about them, as they enjoy the blessedness of a home life together, and may they cling to each other and to You. We ask these things in the name of Jesus Christ our Lord. Amen."

Tassie leaned into the strength of Mitch's arms. Never had she felt so exhilarated, so safe, and so loved.

"Tassie Springer and Mitchell Drummond, you have exchanged your promises and given and received your rings in my presence and in the presence of family and friends. By these acts and declarations you have become husband and wife. According to the power vested in me and the laws of the state of Nebraska, I hereby pronounce you are husband and wife."

Tassie couldn't help but let out a little squeak. *Husband and wife! Mitch and I are officially married!*

"Now if you would turn and face your audience of well-wishers, I would like to introduce you." With a dramatic wave of his arm and smile of sincerity, Chaplain Dale said, "Friends, loved ones, it is my pleasure to introduce Mr. and Mrs. Mitchell Drummond. May God bless their union and bless them as they become a family."

As the strains of the wedding march sounded from the organ, the two made their way out into the foyer, headed toward the life they had just dedicated themselves to—a life centered around their family and God.

A Letter To Our Readers

Dear Reader:

In order that we might better contribute to your reading enjoyment, we would appreciate your taking a few minutes to respond to the following questions. We welcome your comments and read each form and letter we receive. When completed, please return to the following:

Fiction Editor
Heartsong Presents
PO Box 719
Uhrichsville, Ohio 44683

1. Did you enjoy reading *The Preacher Wore a Gun* by Joyce Livingston?
   ❏ Very much! I would like to see more books by this author!
   ❏ Moderately. I would have enjoyed it more if

   _____

   _____

   _____

2. Are you a member of **Heartsong Presents**? ❏ Yes ❏ No
   If no, where did you purchase this book? _____

   _____

3. How would you rate, on a scale from 1 (poor) to 5 (superior), the cover design? _____

4. On a scale from 1 (poor) to 10 (superior), please rate the following elements.

   ____ Heroine   ____ Plot
   ____ Hero   ____ Inspirational theme
   ____ Setting   ____ Secondary characters

5. These characters were special because? _____

_____

_____

6. How has this book inspired your life? _____

_____

_____

7. What settings would you like to see covered in future
   Heartsong Presents books? _____

_____

_____

8. What are some inspirational themes you would like to see
   treated in future books? _____

_____

_____

9. Would you be interested in reading other **Heartsong
   Presents** titles? ❏ Yes   ❏ No

10. Please check your age range:
       ❏ Under 18   ❏ 18-24
       ❏ 25-34   ❏ 35-45
       ❏ 46-55   ❏ Over 55

Name _____

Occupation _____

Address _____

City, State, Zip _____

Heartsong

Any 12
Heartsong
Presents titles
for only
$27.00*

CONTEMPORARY ROMANCE IS CHEAPER BY THE DOZEN!

Buy any assortment of twelve *Heartsong Presents* titles and save 25% off the already discounted price of $2.97 each!

*plus $4.00 shipping and handling per order and sales tax where applicable. If outside the U.S. please call 740–922–7280 for shipping charges.

HEARTSONG PRESENTS TITLES AVAILABLE NOW:

(If ordering from this page, please remember to include it with the order form.)